The Waverly Gallery

A PLAY BY

KENNETH LONERGAN

SAMUEL FRENCH, INC.
45 WEST 25TH STREET   NEW YORK 10010
7623 SUNSET BOULEVARD   HOLLYWOOD 90046
LONDON   TORONTO

ISBN 0 573 62750 9   Printed in U.S.A.   #25628

IMPORTANT BILLING AND CREDIT REQUIREMENTS

All producers of THE WAVERLY GALLERY *must* give credit to the Author of the Play in all programs distributed in connection with performances of the Play and in all instances in which the title of the Play appears for purposes of advertising, publicizing or otherwise exploiting the Play and/or a production. The name of the Author *must* also appear on a separate line, on which no other name appears, immediately following the title, and *must* appear in size of type not less than fifty percent the size of the title type.

In addition, the following credit *must* appear on the main credit page in all programs distributed in connection with performances of the Play:

THE WAVERLY GALLERY was produced on the New York Stage by
Anita Waxman, Elizabeth Williams, Randall L. Wreghitt,
Peggy Lieber, Eric Lieber
in association with Second Stage Theatre.

The World Premiere of THE WAVERLY GALLERY
was originally produced by the
Williamstown Theatre Festival, Michael Ritchie, Producer.

THE PROMENADE THEATRE

Under the Direction of BEN SPRECHER and WILLIAM P. MILLER

ANITA WAXMAN ELIZABETH WILLIAMS RANDALL L. WREGHITT

in association with SECOND STAGE THEATRE

present

EILEEN HECKART

in

THE WAVERLY GALLERY

by KENNETH LONERGAN

with

MAUREEN ANDERMAN ANTHONY ARKIN MARK BLUM JOSH HAMILTON

and starring

SCOTTY BLOCH

as Gladys Green at Wed and Sat Mats

Scenery by	Costumes by	Lighting by
DEREK McLANE	MICHAEL KRASS	KENNETH POSNER

Sound by	Original Music by	Casting by
BRUCE ELLMAN	JASON ROBERT BROWN	AMY CHRISTOPHER

General Manager	Press Representative	Promotions	Production Stage Manager
ALBERT POLAND	BARLOW • HARTMAN public relations	PRO-MARKETING	LLOYD DAVIS, JR.

Directed by

SCOTT ELLIS

The World Premiere of THE WAVERLY GALLERY was originally produced by the WILLIAMSTOWN THEATRE FESTIVAL
MICHAEL RITCHIE, Producer

CHARACTERS

GLADYS GREEN	A former lawyer and Greenwich Village activist, runs a small art gallery, 80s
ELLEN FINE	Her daughter, a psychiatrist, 50s
DANIEL REED	Ellen's son, a speechwriter, 20s
HOWARD FINE	Ellen's husband, Daniel's step-father, a psychiatrist, 50s
DON BOWMAN	A painter and waiter from Lynn, Massachusetts, 30s

SETTING

The play takes place in New York City,
in Greenwich Village and on the Upper West Side of Manhattan,
from 1989 to 1991

PRODUCTION NOTE

For information on speaking the simultaneous dialogue presented
in side-by-side columns, see page 86.

This play is for
my grandmother
and
my mother.

ACT I

Scene 1

(*A tiny gallery in Greenwich Village in the Fall of 1989. GLADYS GREEN and her grandson DANIEL REED sit on either side of GLADYS' desk, eating sandwiches. GLADYS, 80s, is extremely energetic and very hard of hearing. She wears a hearing aid which doesn't do her much good. She is an extraordinarily garrulous, immensely charming and absolutely relentless talker who covers her deep and secret embarrassment at her deafness with even more talking. She lives for company and conversation and perhaps because of her advancing years demands the full attention of her interlocutors with a cheerful and unremitting zeal that can be very wearing after a few minutes. DANIEL, mid-20s, is a very bright, occasionally shy, occasionally sarcastic young man with a sense of humor sometimes described as dry. He is at present giving GLADYS his more or less friendly attention.*)

GLADYS. *I* never knew anything was the matter. Your mother never told me anything. And then one day your father calls me on the phone and says he's coming by to say goodbye and that he's moving out. And I said, "I don't understand! What happened?" But he wouldn't tell me and neither would your mother. I called her and I said "What is the matter?" But she just said that your father had left her and that's all I ever knew about it. We always liked Mark, everybody did, but we felt so bad for him, you know ... his mother was a little kooky, you know? She was charming as hell, but she never knew what to do with him. I *liked* her, but she was a nut, she was *meshugge*. Do you know what that word means?

DANIEL. Yes, I know what it means.

GLADYS. What?

DANIEL . I SAID I KNOW WHAT IT MEANS.

GLADYS. It means kooky, you know: a little nutty — And you know your father never had a real father of his own. But your father and your grandfather, Herb — my husband — were very close. He put your father through medical school, you know —

DANIEL. Yes, I know ...

GLADYS. And he said to your father that he would pay for his medical school whether he married Ellen or not. And he also paid for Mark to be in treatment, you know, with a psychiatrist —

DANIEL. Yeah, I know.

GLADYS. And Mark loved that doctor, but he died too. And your poor father just stood there by the window, crying. I never saw anything like it. He was absolutely heartbroken. Because you know he never had a father of his own, not really. But we always liked Mark. He's a hell of a nice guy, he really is. His mother was witty as hell, but she was a kook, a nut, she was nutty. She had a little magazine, I think, that she used to publish. She was a rather good artist too, and she had a play on Broadway, and she had a very good sense of humor. Oh, she was very charming. But she just didn't know what to do with him. And your mother and father, you know, they were married in that same apartment, in the one, you know, the one in the back, the one you live in. They were married there, did you know that?

DANIEL. Yeah, I did.

GLADYS. What, honey?

DANIEL. YES, I KNEW THAT. I KNEW THAT.

GLADYS. We were very happy in that apartment. You know I built that apartment, when Herb and I — that's Herb, your grandfather, my husband — when we bought the building after we came back from Germany. You know we lived in Germany for two years, before the War, because Herb was studying in a laboratory there —

DANIEL. I know!

GLADYS. Well it's a beautiful apartment. Are you happy there, sweet?

DANIEL. Yes, very happy. I love it.

GLADYS. You love it. Well, that's wonderful. And have you got it all...fixed up the way you like it, honey?

DANIEL. Yes, I just got it painted!

GLADYS. Oh, I haven't seen what you did with it.

DANIEL. Yes you have. You've seen it since then.

GLADYS. What?

DANIEL. YOU'VE SEEN IT.

GLADYS. No, I don't think so.

DANIEL. You've seen it a few times. You don't remember.

GLADYS. Well, maybe I don't remember. But we were very happy there. Do you have a lot of parties?

DANIEL. Once in a while.

GLADYS. You do. Well that's wonderful.

DANIEL. No, once in a while! Not very often!

GLADYS. Well why not? You should have parties, we had parties all the time. We had a New Year's Eve party every year —

DANIEL. Well I'm not as much of a social b —

GLADYS. What?

DANIEL. I'm not as much of a social butterfly as you are!

(She laughs and gives him a friendly slap on the wrist.)

GLADYS. Well why not? Are you shy?

DANIEL. Yeah, I'm a little shy!

GLADYS. You're not shy, are you? Ellen is shy. Your mother is very shy —

DANIEL. Well, she gets it from you!

GLADYS. *(Laughs again.)* From *me*? I was never shy, I love to talk to people! I was never shy! I never understood how your mother can be so shy. She's so beautiful, and she's such a good mother, and she's a damn good doctor. Do you know that, honey?

DANIEL. Yes, I know.

GLADYS. Well your grandfather — that's Herb, your grandfather, my husband — was a doctor too, you know. And he and I were very active in politics at that time. I was with the American Labor Party — Do you know what that is, honey?

DANIEL. Yeah, basically.

GLADYS. — And Emily Bradshaw said that I should run on the ticket for City Council. Did you know that, honey?

DANIEL. Yes!

GLADYS. What?
DANIEL. I said I knew that! Hold on —

(He leans in to adjust her hearing aid.)

GLADYS.	
No! Don't fiddle with it!	
You're gonna break it! What?	DANIEL.
This damn thing is such a	Just wait a minute … hold on.
nuisance — What?	Stop talking — Stop talking for
	a second!

GLADYS.
No! Don't fiddle with it!
You're gonna break it! What?
This damn thing is such a
nuisance — What?

DANIEL.
Just wait a minute … hold on.
Stop talking — Stop talking for
a second!

(He adjusts the hearing aid.)

DANIEL. *(In a normal voice:)* Can you hear me? *(She doesn't hear. He adjusts the hearing aid again. Softly:)* Can you hear me?
GLADYS. I can hear you, yes.

(He sits back. She starts to touch the hearing aid.)

DANIEL. No don't touch it! If you can hear me, leave it alone.

(She obediently puts her hands on the table.)

GLADYS. I won't touch it.
DANIEL. OK.

(She laughs and touches his cheek.)

GLADYS. So are you working hard, honey? Are you working too hard?
DANIEL. Not really.
GLADYS. Are you still … writing for that newspaper?
DANIEL. No, I don't write for a newspaper.
GLADYS. What?
DANIEL. I don't write for the newspaper.
GLADYS. You don't. What do you do?
DANIEL. I write speeches for the Environmental Protection Agency.

GLADYS. Who reads them?

DANIEL. No — I write for a politician, for the local head of the Environmental Protection Agency. It's a government agency —

GLADYS. And do they get — do you get criticisms, critiques of them, do people see them? Who publishes them?

DANIEL. No, they don't get published, somebody *gives* them.... Somebody —

GLADYS. Do you enjoy your work?

DANIEL. Yes, I do.

GLADYS. Well that's wonderful. That's absolutely marvelous. But if you ever need any money, you know you can always ask me, and you don't have to pay it back, in case you ever need some spare cash, and we don't have to say anything to your mother.

DANIEL. No, that's all right. Thank you, but I'm all right.

GLADYS. Well I'd *enjoy* giving it to you! Everybody needs money.

DANIEL. That's true.

GLADYS. What?

DANIEL. I SAID THAT'S TRUE.

GLADYS. Well sure it's true. We always had plenty of money, my father always had plenty of money, and then my brother Harold. But he was a real bastard, you know? Nobody ever liked him. He just didn't know how to get along with people. But if you were ever in trouble, ever in real trouble, he would always lend you money. That's important ...

DANIEL. Sure ...!

GLADYS. Sure. Some people just — they don't know how to get along with people. They just don't know how. They're very troubled. Your father was so charming and so bright — you know he's very smart — but he was very troubled at that time. He couldn't help it. And Ellen was just crazy about him. But she never told me anything. I never knew anything.

DANIEL. I know.

(DANIEL gets up abruptly and comes downstage, addressing the audience directly. Behind him GLADYS slowly cleans up the sandwiches.)

DANIEL. *(To the audience:)* I want to tell you what happened to my grandmother, Gladys Green, near the end of her life. I lived in her building — where I still live — in Greenwich Village, during the last couple of years when she was there. I live in the back apartment. She was in the front, just down the hall. My grandfather — Herb, her husband — died before I was born, and after that she lived with a man named Ronald, but then he died too, and after that she was by herself.

For twenty-eight years she ran a tiny gallery on Waverly Place, around the corner from where we lived. And without being too depressing about it, she didn't always have the best stuff in there. But some of it was pretty good. Most days you could see her in there, watching television or looking out the window. I used to drop by once in a while, but usually if I was walking past the gallery, I'd just duck down behind the cars across the street so she wouldn't see me go by. Until her eyesight got really bad. Then you could just walk right past the window. It's not that I didn't like her. I did. It's just that once you went in there, it was kind of tough getting out again. So I was pretty stingy with the visits.

The last person to have a show there was named Don Bowman, from Massachusetts. He came to the city with an expensive car and no money. He took his pictures into every gallery he could find, until he found my grandmother in the Waverly Gallery off Washington Square.

(DANIEL exits.)

Scene 2

(In the little gallery, GLADYS is looking at DON BOWMAN's portfolio. DON is in his mid-30s, and speaks with a working-class Boston-area accent. He is a little peculiar — and always slightly out of step with those around him; a careful, hard-working and detail-fixated person who devotes a lot of his mental energy to very slowly and carefully arriving at the wrong conclusion.)

GLADYS. You know, these are very good. You're a very good artist.

DON. Yeah, that's my sister. That's her actual wheelchair and that's her in her bedroom. You can't see it, but —

GLADYS. These are absolutely marvelous.

DON. — behind the bureau there's a ramp for her wheelchair, but the bureau interferes with the angle. That's her cat.

GLADYS. And are you — you know, are you showing them around in the art galleries?

DON. That's my mother ...

GLADYS. Another gallery?

DON. *(Not loud enough:)* No, that's my *mother*.

(GLADYS doesn't hear him.)

GLADYS. Uh huh. Well, this show here has been up for a long time — the paintings are by a very talented artist who I've known for years. He lives in Europe now with a man — with his partner. And I told him when he left that I can't keep the pictures up for more than a few weeks, and he said, "That's OK, keep 'em up as long as you want!" *(She laughs.)* But I'm in a jam! Because I don't know what to do with them. I need someone to take them down. I can't do it myself.

DON. Well —

GLADYS. Are you over at — over at the school?

DON. No, no, I'm not at —

GLADYS. Well what's the matter? Don't you think it's a good school?

DON. No, I —

GLADYS. Are you a New Yorker?

DON. No, I'm from New England.

GLADYS. From New England, well it's very pretty up there. My daughter went to medical school in Boston. She lives up by the Park —

DON. Yeah, I'm from just outside of Boston. My mother still lives there. I don't really know anybody in New York. My sister lives in New Jersey —

GLADYS. And my grandson is a — he's — you know, he

writes — articles — for the newspaper. You should show him some of your pictures, maybe he'll — you know, maybe he'll write 'em up for you.

DON. What paper does he write for? *(She doesn't hear.)* What paper does he write for? *(She doesn't hear.)* Does he —

GLADYS. Would you like to put some of your — your pictures up in here? We can put up a few and see what happens.

DON. Oh — Yes ...! Of course! That would be wonderful.

GLADYS. It's not a big place, but it's cute. You know? A lot of students come in here. They look around, and we talk, and a lot of them want to show me their work. There are a lot of good artists around but they don't have anyone to help them. It's not a fancy place, but it's all right.

DON. No, I really like it. It has a lot of character.

GLADYS. I used to have a lot of shows in here, but I have a bad — foot, and I can't walk so well, so I don't come in as much as I used to. I've been on this corner for quite a few years now. I live right around the corner, and my grandson has the apartment in the back. I live in the front.

DON. Uh huh ...

GLADYS. I just walk over from my apartment, and I bring a little — sandwich. I have a little — television, and I like to watch it sometimes. Something's wrong with it so I don't watch it anymore. But I come in and I read the paper, and I always keep that door locked, because you never know who the hell is going to come in these days. This whole neighborhood is changing. This one's sellin' drugs, and that one's tryin' to — get your money — and that one's boppin' people on the head. They have all kinds of signals, they have red hats and blue hats, and you can't tell one from the other, and there are a lot of people now from *South Korea*. They're very well dressed, they've got a lot of money, but that government they have doesn't let them — They don't want to live *there*. They want to come *here*. And the man who runs the hotel likes to have the gallery in the building because people stop by and look in. But he's re-doing the whole place —

DON. Yeah, I saw the hotel was under construc —

GLADYS. Now if you want to put two or three pictures up, you'll have to hang them yourself —

DON. That's no problem —

GLADYS. And if you sell anything, the gallery takes fifty percent of the — of the sale. That's half and half. I don't know what kind of prices you want to charge —

DON. All right. Now if I could —

GLADYS. What?

DON. *(Louder:)* I was just wondering if I could store the rest of the stuff somewhere around here —

GLADYS. Well sure, you can keep them in the back —

DON . — because I been drivin' back and forth to New Jersey and I don't like to have the pictures rattlin' around in the car every day. I work as a waiter up in Lynn, in Massachusetts, and my plan was to come down here and stay with my sister, but she's in a wheelchair, and her house is pretty small, and I didn't realize it's almost a two hour drive each way, so —

GLADYS. Don't you have an apartment?

DON. No, I —

GLADYS. Well you can't sleep on the street!

DON . Well, last night I was too tired to drive all the way back, so I did actually sleep in the car, but —

GLADYS. In the car!

DON. Well the front seat reclines all the way back, so it wasn't really too bad —

GLADYS. Well I'll tell you what. You can buy yourself a little ... cot. And I have a room in the back here, where I keep the pictures. Why don't you get yourself a little — you know, a little fold-out cot, and you can stay in the back there until you get yourself settled in. I only use the place in the day — I live right around the corner — Here, would you like to see it?

DON. Well ... um ...

GLADYS. I don't know if you'll be very comfortable — but it's better than sleeping on the street! Somebody's liable to come along and bop you on the head! This whole neighborhood is changing. There's always some racket outside. They're always setting things off or blowing somethin' up....This used to be a beautiful neighborhood. Now you don't know which one is on drugs and which one is crazy...

(DON follows her as she makes her slow way toward the back.)

DON. Well — if I could really — I mean, if you don't mind, that would be incredibly convenient —

GLADYS. Well why should I mind? I like helping young people. All they want is a little chance. But they don't have anyone to help them.

DON. I mean, eventually it would be great to have a whole show here ...

(GLADYS stops walking so she can talk some more.)

GLADYS. I don't come in very often. I never ran this place to make money. I'm a lawyer for many years, but I don't practice any more. It just gives me something to do. And I enjoy it. I really do. I've had some rather good artists in here.... But if you want, we can take down all these pictures, because the artist is in — in Europe. I'm very angry at him because he left for Europe and he left me all these pictures! I don't know what to do with them. You have to change the show after a while because people walk by and they want to see something new. Do you have enough pictures to put up in here?

DON. Oh I've got more pictures than you want ... *(She doesn't hear. Pause.)* I say, I've probably got more pictures than you want.

GLADYS. Well why shouldn't I want them? I think they show a lot of talent. You're a very talented artist.

DON. Thank you.

Scene 3

(DANIEL enters as the lights cross-fade from the gallery to ELLEN and HOWARD's kitchen across the stage. As DON exits the gallery, ELLEN and HOWARD FINE enter and sit at the kitchen table. They are in their 50s. ELLEN is an Upper West Side psychiatrist and mother, shy with strangers, devoted to her family, but easily frazzled — especially by her mother, and particularly

when she is frightened. HOWARD is a genial, loving, generous man, also a psychiatrist, who prides himself on being straightforward and practical — occasionally to the point of insensitivity.)

[NOTE: When the family speaks to GLADYS they must always speak very loudly and clearly to be heard — but not too loud, or her hearing aid whistles. Unless you are right next her, she cannot really hear a normal tone of voice, even when the hearing aid is functioning properly.]

GLADYS. Hello, honey. *(She grabs his face and kisses it.)* How are you, honey? All right?

DANIEL. Yes, I'm fine thanks.

GLADYS. What?

DANIEL. I said I'm fine!

GLADYS. Good. I'm glad.

DANIEL. Why don't you come in and have some dinner!

GLADYS. What?

DANIEL. I said come eat dinner!

(DANIEL and GLADYS cross toward ELLEN and HOWARD who are at the table, mid-meal.)

GLADYS. All right, honey, what are we having?

DANIEL. I'm not sure. I think we're having meatloaf!

GLADYS. We're not having chicken, are we?

DANIEL. No — we're having meatloaf.

GLADYS. I've had chicken three times already this week.

DANIEL. *(Louder:)* We're not having chicken! We're having MEATLOAF. MEATLOAF.

GLADYS. *(Still not hearing.)* Well, that's all right. Your mother is a wonderful cook. *(DANIEL sits GLADYS at one end of the table, then sits between her and ELLEN. HOWARD is at the other end.)* That whole neighborhood is changing. *(To DANIEL:)* Honey? Do you think the Village has changed much in the last five years?

DANIEL. Yes! It's been changing for a lot longer than that!

GLADYS. The whole place is changing. And there are a lot of

people now from South Korea.

ELLEN. What is this South *Korea* thing?

GLADYS.
They're everywhere you look. They're very well-dressed, and they have a lot of money. They come in the gallery all the time. The whole neighborhood is changing.

DANIEL.
I guess a lot of the NYU students are Asian, but I don't really know ...

DANIEL. Sure!

GLADYS. That bank around the corner used to be a very friendly bank. I knew the manager for many years, and it was always a very friendly place. Now, the whole place, is black. The whole bank. It's all — *black*. And we *wanted* that. We fought for that, for many years. But you go in there and they won't talk to you. I went in and stood there for half an hour and nobody would even talk to me. And there are so many *people* now. That whole neighborhood is changing. Don't you think so, honey?

DANIEL. Yes!

HOWARD. *(To GLADYS, shouting, very loud:)* YES IT'S TOO BAD! IT WAS ONCE A LOVELY NEIGHBORHOOD.

ELLEN. Don't shout please ...

GLADYS. Oh it was a beautiful neighborhood. We were very happy there. Do you have a lot of friends up in — in the country — up — up in — where you go?

ELLEN. Vermont.

GLADYS. What?

ELLEN. We go to Vermont.

GLADYS. And you have a lot of friends there?

ELLEN. No. Not many. A few.

GLADYS. But the people up there know you? And they come around? Do you entertain much up there?

HOWARD. NO WE DON'T LIKE TO HAVE TOO MANY PEOPLE UP THERE, GLADYS!

ELLEN. Howard don't *shout*, it makes it *worse*.

GLADYS. I didn't hear.

DANIEL. He said —

HOWARD. *(Barely lower:)* I SAID, WE GO THERE BECAUSE WE WANT TO GET *AWAY* FROM PEOPLE.

GLADYS. Oh, he's teasing.

HOWARD. *(Still loud:)* NO, WE'RE VERY UNFRIENDLY. WE DON'T LIKE TO SEE TOO MANY PEOPLE.

GLADYS. *(To DANIEL:)* He's teasing you.

HOWARD. WHEN YOU HAD — LISTEN: WHEN YOU HAD THE HOUSE ON FIRE ISLAND ALL THOSE YEARS, YOU LIKED TO ENTERTAIN ALL THE TIME —

GLADYS. Well sure, everybody likes to have parties

HOWARD. BUT WE DON'T ENJOY THAT THE WAY YOU DID! WE LOVE THE COUNTRY AND WE LIKE THE SCENERY, BUT WE DON'T LIKE HAVING A LOT OF PEOPLE UP THERE BECAUSE WE SEE TOO MANY PEOPLE HERE IN THE CITY.

GLADYS. Well sure, everybody likes to see people — We used to have people all the time when we went to Fire Island.

HOWARD. RIGHT!

GLADYS. We had a beautiful house there and we entertained quite a lot.

HOWARD. RIGHT! WE DON'T LIKE THAT!

GLADYS. Well, it's a beautiful place. *(To DANIEL:)* Honey, do you want some of these — potatoes?

DANIEL. *(Very loud:)* NO THANK YOU.

ELLEN. Danny, you don't have to shout — There she goes. *(GLADYS is fiddling with her hearing aid.)* Don't touch your hearing aid —

GLADYS. It's whistling —

ELLEN. *(Getting up.)* Just a minute — Don't touch it —

(She comes around and adjusts the hearing aid.)

ELLEN.	GLADYS.
Don't hold it with your — All you have to do is — All you have to do is touch it with your finger — Don't grab the knob —	There's a terrible whistling. Can you hear that? Does anybody hear that whistling?

ELLEN. *(Continued.)*
Howard it's too *small* for her, she can't get her finger on it — J —

HOWARD.
Honey, why don't you do it *for* her?

(ELLEN patiently adjusts the hearing aid.)

GLADYS. *(Laughs nervously.)* What a crazy business!
HOWARD. Daniel, pass me the potatoes.

(DANIEL passes the potatoes.)

ELLEN. *(In a normal voice:)* Can you hear me?
HOWARD. *(Takes potatoes.)* Thank you.

(ELLEN readjusts the hearing aid.)

ELLEN. *(In a normal voice:)* Can you hear me?
GLADYS. Yes. Perfect.

(She immediately starts to touch the hearing aid.)

ELLEN.
No don't touch it anymore — !

DANIEL.
Leave it alone if you can hear!

GLADYS. Up! I won't go near it! *(They resume eating.)* You know, Ellen, that one in the gallery, that young artist, has got a sister somewhere who's in a wheelchair, and a mother in — you know, where you go — in the country —
HOWARD. NO, GLADYS, WE GO TO VERMONT! HE'S FROM MASSACHUSETTS!

ELLEN.
Howard don't *shout* at her!

DANIEL.
You don't have to shout!

GLADYS. Oh, he's from Massachusetts? I didn't know that.
ELLEN. Yes you did. But you forgot.

GLADYS. What?

HOWARD. SOMETIMES YOUR MEMORY ISN'T SO GOOD.

GLADYS. *(Hearing but ignoring this comment.)* Ellen, this dinner is absolutely delicious.

ELLEN. Thank you.

GLADYS. Absolutely marvelous. *(Pushing a dish of broccoli.)* Does anybody want any of this? Honey? Do you want any of this — vegetable? It's very good.

DANIEL. No, I've got some of my own right here, thanks!

GLADYS. Do you want some?

DANIEL. No I HAVE SOME. THANK YOU!

(GLADYS offers DANIEL some soda.)

GLADYS. Would you like some of this drink?

DANIEL. NO THANKS!

ELLEN. Volume.

DANIEL.	GLADYS.
Sorry. Sorry.	It has a very good — flavor. Go ahead and try some. I can't drink all of this.

DANIEL. No thank you.

ELLEN. *(Under her breath:)* "Can you cook?"

GLADYS. This dinner is absolutely delicious.

ELLEN. No one could accuse her of being unappreciative.

HOWARD. *(To DANIEL:)* Are you still seeing that same horrible girl?

GLADYS. Do you know how to cook, honey?

DANIEL. *(To HOWARD:)* Um — I don't really know. I —

GLADYS. *(To DANIEL:)* Did you ever learn to cook?

DANIEL. A little bit!

(GLADYS cheers and claps her hands.)

GLADYS. You do? Well good for you! Are you a good cook?

HOWARD. *(To DANIEL:)* Is that not a suitable subject for conversation?

DANIEL. *(To HOWARD:)* Um — *(Turns to GLADYS.)* I can only cook a little bit! I can't really cook —

GLADYS. Well who taught you how?

DANIEL. I taught myself!

HOWARD. Dan? Is that not a suitable subject for conversation?

GLADYS. And do you ever have friends over and — you know — cook 'em up something to eat?

DANIEL. *(To HOWARD:)* No, it doesn't matter. I don't care. She's driving me crazy, that's all.

GLADYS. What's the matter, honey?

DANIEL. Nothing!

HOWARD. Why do you go out with all these crazy girls?

DANIEL. I don't know.

GLADYS. I never learned how to cook. I never used to cook anything.

HOWARD.
Well as you know, I hate to butt in, but there are several perfectly nice young ladies at the Institute. I'd be happy to fix you up with one if you're interested.

DANIEL.
I don't know — I don't really want to —

HOWARD.
Well ... It's just a suggestion. ... It's too bad you're shy about that sort of thing.

DANIEL.
Yeah, well ... I ... I just ... I don't know. I'm not really —

HOWARD.
It's fine, sweetheart. Just let me know if you're interested.

ELLEN.
Interested in what?

GLADYS.
We had a woman who used to come in and cook for us. *(Pause.)* Ellen, do you remember Fanny? ... Ellen, do you remember Fanny?

ELLEN. *(Quietly:)*
Yes.

GLADYS.
You don't remember her.

ELLEN.
Of course I remember her ...!

GLADYS.
She was a marvelous cook. She used to cook everything. I never learned how. I never liked to cook.

HOWARD.
I offered to fix him up with
one of the young single
women at the Institute.

ELLEN.
Oh...!

HOWARD.
There's a very nice young lady in
my program who mentioned to me
that she'd like to meet somebody,
and I —

ELLEN.
Howard — I can't listen to six
different people talking to me
at the same time — !

GLADYS.
Ellen, I want to bring — that young
artist, the one who's having a show
— the — the one —

DANIEL.
Don!

GLADYS.
Don. Should I ask him to come
up here next week?

Ellen? You know what I think
I'll do.

Ellen? You know what I think
I'll do?

HOWARD. *(To ELLEN:)* Sorry.

GLADYS. … I'm gonna bring that young artist up with me next week so you can meet him.

ELLEN. Please don't! I don't need anybody new to cook for!

GLADYS. What?

ELLEN. DON'T bring him up next week, I don't want to cook DINNER for everybody! We'll meet him on Saturday. DON'T invite him for dinner!

GLADYS. Don't invite him. Well, that's fine. I don't need to invite him, I don't need to invite anybody. I thought you might want to meet him. He's a very interesting guy.

ELLEN. We will meet him on Saturday.

GLADYS. What?

ELLEN. We will meet him on SATURDAY.

GLADYS. He's from the same place, you know, where you go up — on the weekend —

ELLEN. She's getting worse.

DANIEL. Oh she's definitely getting worse, Mom.

GLADYS. What's the matter, honey?

DANIEL. Nothing! Everything's fine! Do you want some more?

GLADYS. Oh! No! I couldn't eat another thing.

ELLEN. "You got any coffee lying around?"

GLADYS. Ellen, is there any coffee lying around?

ELLEN. Not yet! I'm just about to make some!

GLADYS. Does anybody else want any? Honey, do you like coffee?

DANIEL. Yes I do.

GLADYS. Are you a coffee lover?

DANIEL. Yes I am. I'm a coffee lover.

GLADYS. Where's the dog?

ELLEN. I'm going to blow my brains out.

DANIEL. The dog is in the other room!

GLADYS. What's the matter? Is she hiding?

DANIEL. She's waiting for food.

GLADYS. What's the matter? Didn't anybody feed her?

ELLEN. No, we're going to let her starve!

HOWARD. Honey, please — before we all go insane.

GLADYS. Shouldn't somebody give her something?

ELLEN. DON'T GIVE HER ANYTHING, SHE'S NOT SUP-POSED TO BEG!

GLADYS. Ohhhhhh, poor thing, she must be hungry.

ELLEN.	DANIEL.
Please don't feed her anything!	She's fine! She was just fed!
She's not supposed to beg.	She just ate a little while ago!

GLADYS. That dog is just the sweetest little animal. Do you take her up with you when you go away to — when you go up to —

DANIEL, HOWARD and ELLEN. Vermont!

GLADYS. Is that where it is?

DANIEL. *(Getting up.)* I have to take a break.

GLADYS. Where you going, hon?

DANIEL. In the living room.

GLADYS. What?

DANIEL. *(Leans in, speaks softly:)* In the living room.

GLADYS. Does anybody want any coffee?

ELLEN. I'm just *making* it! Give me five minutes to make it...!

DANIEL. I'll make it.

(ELLEN walks out.)

> GLADYS. What's the matter? What's wrong with Ellen?
> DANIEL. Nothing!
> HOWARD. She's just tired!

(DANIEL laughs.)

> GLADYS. Ohhhhhh, poor Ellen. Is she working too hard? I think she works too hard. Your mother works harder than anyone I know. She's always working.
> HOWARD. Gladys, millions of people work very hard, every day, all day long!
> DANIEL. What are you trying to do, improve her character?
> HOWARD. *(Shrugs.)* Sure!
> GLADYS. You got any coffee lyin' around?
> DANIEL. I'm just about to make it!

(He goes around the corner to make coffee.)

> GLADYS. You know, I told that young artist that he should get himself … should get himself a little — cot, and put it in the back room —
> ELLEN. *(Off.)* Howard will you *say* something to her about that?

HOWARD.	GLADYS. *(Continued:)*
Honey, what do you want me to say?	— so he won't have to drive all the way every day. He doesn't
ELLEN. *(Off.)*	know a soul in the city, and I
Tell her she can't let him *do*	I said, "Well you can't stay
that until we at least *meet*	with *me*, there's no room in that
him --	apartment —" What's the matter?
HOWARD.	
Why don't *you* tell her?	
ELLEN. *(Off.)*	
Because I've told her five	
times already —	

(DANIEL reappears, eating ice cream out of the carton.)

GLADYS. What's the matter, honey?

DANIEL. Nothing!

GLADYS. This young artist is about the same age as you are — and I think he's very talented. He works like hell on those pictures and he has a very charming personality

HOWARD. LISTEN: WE WANT TO MEET HIM BEFORE YOU LET HIM MOVE IN THE BACK OF THE GALLERY.

GLADYS. Well you *will* meet him. What's the matter?

HOWARD. BECAUSE, GLADYS —

GLADYS. His mother doesn't live in the city. And I don't think she wants him to be here. I think she's a real nut case.

HOWARD. Gladys —

GLADYS. And I think she's —

HOWARD. — GLADYS — LISTEN TO ME.

GLADYS. Yes.

HOWARD. WE DON'T WANT YOU TO AGREE —

ELLEN. *(Off.)* Don't *shout!*

HOWARD. Honey, I can't *help* it!

ELLEN. *(Off.)* It's too *loud* for her, Howard!

HOWARD. *(Slightly lower:)* Gladys, don't tell him he can stay there until we meet him and make sure everything's all right!

GLADYS. I already told him if he wants —

HOWARD. No, Gladys! Listen to me! I'm sure he's very nice, but it's not appropriate to have him stay there until we make sure there's nothing peculiar about him.

GLADYS. Well why should he have to lug that car all around when nobody's in that room all day long —

HOWARD. *(On "nobody's:")* It's not appropriate to have a stranger sleeping in the back of the gallery if you don't know anything about him.

GLADYS. But he's not living with *me. I* don't want that, I'm not lookin' for that anymore...!

HOWARD. I understand that. And I'm also sure he's perfectly harmless. But until we meet him, you still have to tell him he's going to have to make some other arrangement.

ELLEN. *(Off.)* How is she going to do that? She can't even remember his *name.*

HOWARD.   GLADYS.
Then *you* tell her, because I —   What's the matter?
(To GLADYS:) Nothing! Just do   What's wrong?
what you're told. You know
how to do that.

GLADYS. I always do what I'm told!
HOWARD. Right! Except when you don't want to!
GLADYS. Well what's wrong with that?

(Everyone laughs.)

HOWARD. Just wait until we meet him! And don't argue!
GLADYS. All right, who's arguing?
DANIEL. *(Eating ice cream.)* Mom, do you want any ice cream?
ELLEN. *(Off.)* No thank you.
DANIEL. Well, I'm going to finish it …
ELLEN. *(Off.)* Be my guest.

(GLADYS hums to herself because no one is talking to her.)

HOWARD. Is this girl you're seeing also involved in politics?
DANIEL. I'm not actually seeing her, she can't make up her mind whether or not I'm seeing her ...
HOWARD. Is she involved in politics?
DANIEL. No, she's involved in torture. She comes over and she tortures me and then she goes away and looks around for somebody to torture her — which she actually seems to prefer — but she has extremely high standards, so if she's can't find anyone sufficiently diabolical, she comes back and tortures me some more.
HOWARD. Jesus Christ. She sounds delightful.
DANIEL. Oh she's great.

(ELLEN enters and goes to GLADYS.)

ELLEN. *(Softly:)* Why don't you go sit in the living room and I'll bring you some coffee?
GLADYS. Ellen? Can I do something in here? Do you want me

to do the dishes?

ELLEN. No thanks. There's nothing to do.

(GLADYS hums to herself again under the following:)

DANIEL. Anyway, it doesn't matter because she's going to Turkey next week anyway.

ELLEN. Turkey! What's she doing in Turkey?

DANIEL. I don't know. Traveling around. Lecturing at a torture symposium, I don't know.

ELLEN	HOWARD
Well maybe she'll stay there.	Good! Maybe she'll emigrate!

GLADYS. Ellen, can I help clean off the table?

ELLEN. No thank you. It's almost done.

(ELLEN goes around the corner.)

HOWARD. Is this girl in analysis?

DANIEL. Yes, unfortunately her analyst recently committed suicide.

HOWARD. He did? No ...

DANIEL. Yes that's the third psychoanalyst who tried to treat her and ended up killing himself. She's cutting a swath of terror through the New York Psychoanalytic Institute. I'm surprised you guys haven't seen anything about it in *The Psychoanalytic Quarterly*.

HOWARD. *(Laughing.)* Come on...!

DANIEL. *(Laughing.)* It's true — They say she has no super-ego. They're dropping like flies.

(They laugh. GLADYS smiles.)

GLADYS. What's he laughing at, honey? What's he laughing at? What's everybody laughing at?

DANIEL. Nothing, nothing, it's not important.

(He starts reading a section of the newspaper. HOWARD eats a cookie. After a moment, GLADYS resumes humming to herself.)

Scene 4

(The gallery. HOWARD is talking to DON. DANIEL is looking at the pictures.)

DON. Oh yeah, she's a terrific lady. Only I don't think that hearing aid of hers is very powerful because I often have to repeat myself when I'm talkin' to her. But she is extremely sharp. You can see that right away —

HOWARD. Yes she is, in her own inimitable fashion —

DON. But I can see where it's already kind of frustrating — because you know, like, the other day: I was movin' my car — That's my car right out front there — the maroon one, the Lincoln — and when I come back, Gladys says to me there was a couple in here and they want to buy a picture...!

HOWARD. Oh — !

DON. So I'm thinkin' "Terrific!" I been in New York City two weeks, I got my pictures up in a gallery in Greenwich Village, and I just sold my first picture!

HOWARD. Congratulations!

DON. Wait — that's not the end of it. Because it turns out she didn't get a *name.*

HOWARD. *(Smiles to DANIEL.)* Jesus Christ ...

DON. I *think,* because she couldn't hear them. And I almost tear the place apart lookin' for a scrap of paper or something in case she wrote it down, and don't you know it: No name, no paper, and I'm still waitin' for 'em. They sure haven't been back yet.

HOWARD. I'm afraid that's more her memory than her hearing aid ...

DON. Well, she remembers stuff, but plenty of times I'll say something to her and I can tell, kinda *tell* she didn't really hear me, but she doesn't want to let on. So I think it's the hearing aid problem more than anything else.... They make some pretty good ones now. I don't know what kind she's got now, but boy, it'd be great if somebody could get her a better one. Because God only knows how many pictures I really sold, if you see what I mean. But I'm not complaining. She's a great lady, but she's just kinda stubborn.

(ELLEN comes in from the street.)

HOWARD. Yes she is. *(To ELLEN:)* Hello there.

ELLEN . Hello. *(She sits.)* Blurf. What a day.

DON. Everything all right?

ELLEN. Oh, fine. *(Turns to HOWARD.)* Howard, I made her show me how she does her insulin, and she's been — she sticks the needle *through* the gauze pad, and then she pulls plunger *up* — so all she does is fill the syringe with blood, and then she throws it away. So —

HOWARD.	DANIEL.
For Christ's sake ...	I'm amazed she can even *see* that needle.

ELLEN. *(Continued:)* — for all I know she hasn't taken it for *days*. *Weeks*, for all I know.

HOWARD. Well, maybe we should —

ELLEN. — I'm going to have Florence do it when she comes in the mornings, but she's only there twice a week. We're gonna have to get someone to come in the rest of the time. It doesn't seem to be *killing* her, but ...

DON. What's wrong, she has diabetes?

ELLEN. Yes, very mild — she takes *this* much insulin in the mornings. *(Indicates tiny amount.)* But you still have to do it every day. I'm gonna talk to Dr. Wagner again ... *(Pause.)* That *sign* of hers outside is really crummy looking. It's half *off*. I'm gonna call my cousin Bill.

DANIEL. Hey, did you see the renovations they're doing in the hotel?

HOWARD. Oh yes ...

ELLEN. Yes, he's really jazzing it up. I looked inside. They've got a new floor and an iron — gate — or trellis or something. It actually looks rather nice.

DANIEL. Yeah, the whole lobby was like *rubble* for about six months, but now it looks pretty good —

HOWARD. *(To DON:)* The hotel this gallery is a part of used to be the seediest, most God-awful place —

ELLEN. That's not true. When I was growing up it was very nice. It was a nice, rather quaint, residential Greenwich Village hotel ...

DON. Is there somethin' wrong with the guy who runs it? Gladys ...

ELLEN. Oh —

HOWARD. No, that's just —

ELLEN. — He snubbed her, or she thinks he snubbed her, or maybe he said hello and she didn't *hear* him ... I don't know. Anyway ...

HOWARD. Anyway, that was *it. Criminal.*

ELLEN. Well *I* don't know. Maybe he *was* rude to her. I think he's a little peculiar.

DON. Yeah I met that guy, the owner — Mr. Georgio? Georgianni?

ELLEN. George. Alan George.

DON. I thought he was Italian.

ELLEN. I don't think so ...

DON. "Georgio." That sounds Italian.

ELLEN.	DANIEL.
... Unless he changed his name or something.	I thought he was Jewish. He's Jewish, that guy.

HOWARD. They probably changed it at Ellis Island, like everyone else. Right?

DON. Are you all Jewish?

(Pause.)

ELLEN.	DANIEL.
Well — yes ...	I'm half-Jewish. But since my
HOWARD. *(To DAN:)*	my mother's Jewish, that means
You're Jewish. You're Jewish.	I'm Jewish — by ancient Jewish
Jewish. You're *Jewish.*	law.

ELLEN. We're not very religious.

HOWARD. What do you mean we're not very religious? We're

not religious at *all*. Except *I* was raised —

DANIEL. We're liberal Upper West Side atheistic Jewish intellectuals — and we really like German choral music.

(ELLEN and HOWARD laugh.)

DON. My family's not very religious either. Well, I suppose my father was, in a way, but not really.... He used to drag me kickin' and screamin' to Church every Sunday, but my mother always stayed at home ...

(Silence.)

HOWARD. Actually, it's very interesting: Gladys' father was from Russia, where he was a book-maker for the Czar —

ELLEN.	DANIEL
Book-*binder*, Howard. He wasn't —	He was a book-*binder*. It wasn't like he was the Czar's *bookie*.

HOWARD. Yes, excuse me, book-binder for the Czar. And he came here in the teens, I think, or possibly earlier —

ELLEN. Oh, I think earlier, Howard —

HOWARD. And he founded a very successful publishing business by carting Jewish religious books around the Lower East Side in a wheelbarrow —

DON. Really.

HOWARD. Until Gladys' nephew took it over from *his* father and proceeded to run it into the ground. Right? Schmuck!

DON. No, I didn't know that —

ELLEN.	HOWARD.
And my mother —	And Gladys thinks it's all bullshit.

ELLEN. Yes, my whole childhood I was raised to think that anybody who was religious at *all* was some kind of *moron*.

HOWARD. Gladys is very broadminded.

ELLEN. Well, she was always —

HOWARD. Right? Like a good communist.

ELLEN. Well she *was* a communist. I spent my whole childhood listening to her and my father and their friends argue *politics* all night long. My father would sit there and play devil's advocate to all my mother's friends, they'd have screaming fights until two in the morning and then she'd get up at the crack of dawn to go stand on a milk carton in Washington Square and campaign for low-income housing. She was very impressive in her own maddening way. But those discussions used to drive me *crazy* ...

HOWARD. Really? I always thought you enjoyed them.

ELLEN. Ha ha.

HOWARD. *(To DON.)* But I'll tell you, if you ever wanted anything done in New York, you called Gladys.

ELLEN. Oh yes.

DANIEL. Oh yeah.

HOWARD. An apartment, a *job*, a lawyer ...

ELLEN. A moving company — Remember she used to hire those crazy Israeli movers...?

DANIEL. I remember them.

ELLEN. One of them was a *sculptor* and one was a *musician* ...

DANIEL. Yeah. Mom, they were both *insane*.

HOWARD. *(To DON:)* When I was divorced from my first wife, I called Gladys and I told her I needed an apartment, and in *twenty-four hours* she found me a wonderful little apartment on 86th street, right across the Park from where my children were living, with a separate office space so I could see patients — and half a block from the Park so I could walk my dog.

DON. Really.

HOWARD. ...It was amazing!

ELLEN. *(To HOWARD and DON:)* She was very good at that ...

DANIEL. *(To DON:)* When I was a little kid she was always going off on these trips around the world — She took me to the Yucatan when I was ten so I could see the pyramids —

HOWARD. ...And by the time she got off the boat she'd know everybody on board, she'd know everything about them ...

ELLEN. Right, and then she'd bring them all back to New York and invite them over so I could cook dinner for them.

HOWARD. *(To ELLEN:)* A lot's changed in twenty years, kid!

ELLEN. And then she'd take *Zique (Pronounced like "Zeke.")* with her.

DANIEL. She used to have this psychotic Dalmatian —

ELLEN. Zique!

HOWARD. Which is spelled —

ELLEN.	HOWARD. *(On "Q".)*
Z. I. Q. U. E. for some reason.	Z. I. Q. U. E.

DANIEL. — who used to hide under the table when anybody came into the room.

ELLEN. And who she used to take on these cruises where they didn't allow dogs —

DANIEL. And she'd say —

ELLEN. "Oh, they don't allow dogs on that boat but I just take her anyway —

DANIEL and ELLEN. " — *They* don't mind."

HOWARD. *(To DON:)* This was the craziest fuckin' dog you ever met.

ELLEN. *(To HOWARD:)* Right, because *you* told her to get her.

HOWARD. I didn't tell her to get *Zique*.

ELLEN.	DANIEL.
You did too!	Yes you did!

HOWARD. *(To DON:)* I told Gladys I thought she should get a dog —

ELLEN. Boy was she mad at you.

HOWARD. — because at the time, we were worried about her being in the gallery by herself with all the crazies running around ...

DANIEL. The worst thing that's gonna happen to her in this neighborhood is that somebody's gonna try to sell her *pot*.

ELLEN. *(To HOWARD:)* Right, and she got very offended ...

HOWARD. Right, she got very offended ...

ELLEN. ...Because you called her a little old lady ...

HOWARD. Because I told her I didn't think it was such a great idea for a little old lady to sit by herself in the window all day long, when you've got —

ELLEN. And was she mad!

HOWARD. What can I say? I was my usual tactful self.

ELLEN. ...and this was fifteen *years* ago.

DANIEL. ... yeah, so you said she should get an *attack* dog.

HOWARD. I didn't say an *attack* dog. Come on!

ELLEN	DANIEL
Yes you *did*, Howard!	Yes you did! You said she should get a German Shepherd!

HOWARD. *(To DANIEL, on "German:")* I told her to get a *dog*, in case some lunatic walks in, she should have a dog who's gonna bark at them and scare them away. (To DON:) Right? So she goes to the pound —

DANIEL.	HOWARD.
And she comes back with —	— and she comes back with this skinny little cadaverous Dalmatian —

DANIEL. Who *shakes*!

HOWARD. — who shakes, and hides under the table every time you come into the room!

(ELLEN, DANIEL and HOWARD are all laughing.)

DON. That's funny ...

HOWARD. ... so I said "Gladys, what the hell are you *doing*? That dog wouldn't scare *any*body!"

ELLEN. ... She was very fond of her.

HOWARD. Listen, it was a wonderful thing for her.

ELLEN. Zique wasn't so bad. She just shook.

DANIEL. Unbelievable.

(Silence.)

HOWARD. *(To DON:)* Well...you don't seem too dangerous.
DON. Oh … Thank you.

(Pause.)

HOWARD.	DON.
So —	Now all you gotta do is tell that Mr. Georgio.

ELLEN. Oh no don't worry about him. I don't think he ever comes in here.
DON. Oh, he was sure in here the other day. And I don't think he was too happy about my bein' here ...

(Pause. ELLEN and HOWARD look at each other and then back at DON.)

ELLEN. Oh really?
HOWARD. Really?

(Pause. DON is a bit taken aback.)

DON. Well, yeah —

DANIEL.	ELLEN.
Why? What did he say?	Did he say anything to you?

DON. Oh no, he just —
ELLEN. I didn't think he ever came *in* here ...
DON. No, he's been in here a couple of times. He —
ELLEN . My mother always thought he was rather strange.
HOWARD. What did he say?
DON. I don't remember exactly. I didn't talk to him for very long ...
ELLEN. Well, I don't see why he should mind ...
DANIEL. Yeah, what does he care?

HOWARD. Listen, he's probably just being a pain in the ass.

DON. I don't know — He's probably worried somebody's gonna see me in here late at night and think I'm tryin' to rob the place.

DANIEL. Rob it of what?

HOWARD. No — That's crazy.

DANIEL. What would you steal?

DON. No, I could see his point. Somebody could come in at night and try to steal my pictures off the wall.

(Pause.)

DANIEL. What do mean, like, Art Thieves?

HOWARD. No ...

DON. It could happen.

DANIEL. I don't think so.

HOWARD. It's highly unlikely.

ELLEN. I'll give him a call on Monday. But I don't see why he should have any objection —

DON. Yeah, he probably had a bee in his bonnet about something else.... He said he was gonna talk to Gladys, so he probably straightened it out with her.

DANIEL. *(A joke:)* Oh yes. I'm sure she cleared everything right up.

HOWARD. At any rate, I don't think we have to worry about that now ...

ELLEN. I'll give him a call.... I hope that's not going to be a problem.

HOWARD. I don't think so, honey. *(To DON.)* Listen: I think we'd like to buy one of your pictures.

DON. Oh — ! That's great. Wow. That's — OK, fantastic.

HOWARD. My oldest son is having a birthday next week, and his wife is expecting a baby, and I think one of these would make a terrific birthday gift.

DON. Great. Uh —

HOWARD. *(Pointing.)* I like this one. Do you like this one, sweetheart?

ELLEN. *(Looking.)* Ooh, yes.

DON. Oh yeah, that's a little wharf in my home town. I tried really hard to get in all the details. This guy here runs a bait and tackle store. And these birds — the birds come and sit on top of this guy's sign all day long. Drives him nuts, 'cause — well, you know, 'cause they deface the sign. So he's always out there cleaning it off. I didn't put that in. I tried to be faithful to what's actually there, otherwise ...

HOWARD.	
Sold. Sold. Now, I notice you	
don't have any prices on these ...	DON.
How about...Is three hundred	Oh, well, I, uh...
dollars … fair?	

DON. *(Disappointed.)* Oh. Sure. Absolutely. That's great....You know, you're Gladys's family....Three hundred — that's more than fair. That's one of my favorites. And that's — a nice — uh — frame you're gettin', too —

HOWARD. And listen: You don't have to worry about Gladys forgetting our names! Right?

DON. Right. Right.

ELLEN. *(Cheerfully.)* I remember when she *got* this place.

Scene 5

(As DANIEL comes forward and addresses the audience, ELLEN's kitchen lights up. ELLEN talks on the phone silently, slowly turning her back to us.)

DANIEL. *(To the audience.)* My mother called Mr. George who said he had no problem with Don staying in the gallery. So Don moved into the little room in the back — which was basically a closet — he moved his car around, he walked my grandmother back and forth from the house, and sometimes he cooked her lunch. Late at night if you looked past the drug dealers on the corner, you could usually see Don through the gallery window, hovering over his pictures, touching them up with a little brush.

My mother hired a nurses' aid named Marva to come in the mornings when Florence wasn't there, to give Gladys breakfast and help with her insulin. She hated it. She said there were these *women* in the house and they wouldn't go away. Mom took her to the eye doctor and the ear doctor. Paid her bills, paid her taxes. I dropped by her apartment to say hello once in a while. I let her take me to dinner once a month at the restaurant next door. They were really nice to her there, so she really liked that. She rang my doorbell, a lot. Sometimes I was nice to her. Sometimes I yelled at her. And she went to the gallery, almost every day. Until winter came and she stopped going to the gallery for the time being because she couldn't stand the cold. She just stayed in her apartment with those *women* and we waited for the spring.

Then in January, Mr. George called my mother and told her he was taking away the gallery and turning it into a breakfast cafe for his hotel.

(DANIEL turns and enters the kitchen.)

ELLEN. Anyway —
DANIEL. What did he say?
ELLEN. He says he's turning the gallery into a cafe and connecting it to the rest of the hotel, and he wants her to be out by the end of May.
DANIEL. The end of *May*? He's got to be kidding.
ELLEN. I *knew* something like this would happen ...
DANIEL. Well can't he — I mean, can't we — Can he *do* that? Doesn't he have to —
ELLEN. Well honey, she doesn't even have a lease.
DANIEL. She doesn't have a *lease*?
ELLEN. No, she always said she —
DANIEL. She's been in there for twenty eight years and she doesn't have a lease?
ELLEN. No. And you know, I asked him if it was because Don's been in there for so long and he said "Oh no, it's got nothing to do

with that — " But maybe he thinks she's peculiar, sitting there all day long … and then Don's in there at night…. I don't know, maybe it's no good for his new … I don't really know. He obviously — he's having plans drawn up, so … *(Pause.)* It's just — if he kicks her out I don't know what she's going to *do*.

(Pause.)

DANIEL. How can she not have a lease?

ELLEN. I don't know. She used to say she didn't want a lease because then he could raise the rent.

DANIEL. What?

ELLEN. I don't *know*. Nobody ever used that space. It's not even attached to the rest of the hotel. But he wants to knock a wall down and put in a kitchen and use it as a breakfast cafe for the hotel.

DANIEL. Well can't she … *(Pause.)* I mean, what if we say no? What can he —

ELLEN. Well I thought of that, honey, but if she has no lease there's really not much we can do about it. We could refuse to get out, but then he could start sending in process servers and people to harass her and I don't want that …

DANIEL. No …

ELLEN. … She wouldn't know what was going on.

DANIEL. Serve somebody right if he sent them in there after her, they'd run out screaming.

ELLEN. *(Short laugh.)* Right.

GLADYS. *(Off.)* Ellen? Ellen?

DANIEL. What is she gonna *do*?

ELLEN. I don't know.

GLADYS. *(Off.)* Hello? Hello? Ellen? Where are you? Where'd you go?

(ELLEN goes out.)

ELLEN. *(Off.)*	GLADYS. *(Off.)*
I'm just in the kitchen! I'm just ta — I'm just talking to Danny about something!	Where were you, honey? What's the matter?

GLADYS. *(Off.)* What's the matter? Is he crying?

DANIEL. *(To himself:)* Am I what?

ELLEN. *(Off.)* No! Why would he be crying?

GLADYS. *(Off.)* I don't know. I thought somebody was crying.

ELLEN. *(Off.)* You were probably having a dream! Why don't you sit here and in a few minutes I'll bring you something to drink!

GLADYS. *(Off)* All right. I'll stay here.

(ELLEN enters.)

ELLEN. You don't look like you're crying.

DANIEL. Mom, this is really bad.

ELLEN. Well, I can ask Arthur if he knows some kind of fancy legal maneuver, but I'm pretty sure there's nothing to be done.

DANIEL. Yeah, because maybe — don't they have to give notice, or something?

ELLEN. He's giving us five months.

DANIEL. Five months.

ELLEN. She doesn't even go there in the winter. I don't think she's been in there since November. She just sits, all day long in that tiny little apartment. *You're* busy, and I can't have her up here more than once or twice a week or I go out of my mind. She complained to me all last winter how she's lonely, she's lonely — well she *is* very lonely. She won't read — or she *can't* read — And Florence — who's a *saint*, says she can't even figure out how to work the television.... What's she going to *do* all day long? *(Pause.)* And *I* feel bad for *you.* I only get it twice a week, but you're on the front lines —

DANIEL. Listen — I'm not —

ELLEN. You can't spend your life running around taking care of her. Karl says he went in yesterday and she was asleep on the sofa ...

DANIEL. Yeah I know, you told me.

ELLEN. And she had left the coffee pot lying on its side on the burner and the entire apartment was filled with smoke ...

DANIEL. I know. You *told* me.

ELLEN. I'm afraid one of these days she's going to burn the whole house down. *(Pause.)* He's got some fuckin' nerve kicking her out of that gallery for his — fuckin' hotel expansions.

DANIEL. I know …!

ELLEN. I mean, eventually she's going to have to move in here, but I'm dreading that day. Because when she does, *I'm* going to have to move *out*.

DANIEL. Well —

ELLEN. *(Her voice suddenly catches.)* Do you know what she said to me last week? *(Pause.)* She wants to get a job in a *law* firm. Did I know anybody who she could work for as a *lawyer*. *(Pause.)* And now Don's on her shit list because he wants to visit his mother again —

DANIEL. Yeah I know, she gave me a whole long monologue about that recently —

(ELLEN sees something, gets up and walks out.)

ELLEN. *(Off.)* PLEASE DON'T FEED THE DOG!

GLADYS. *(Off.)* But she's so hungry — !

ELLEN. *(Off.)* I'M GOING TO FEED HER DINNER IN A FEW MINUTES! DON'T FEED HER, SHE'S NOT SUPPOSED TO BEG!

GLADYS. *(Off.)* Well what are you so angry about?

DANIEL. Mom …!

(ELLEN stalks in with a plate of crackers and cheese. She clatters it down on the table.)

ELLEN. Howard thinks we should get her a cat.

DANIEL. A cat?

ELLEN. Well, you don't have to walk a cat, and you can leave its food out all day long, and it shits in a cat box, and she's so fond of Daisy, so maybe it's not such a terrible idea. She can feed it all day long until it explodes. She'll love it.

DANIEL. Yeah but what happens if she opens her door at night and it runs out? How's she gonna get it back?

ELLEN. I don't know.… That's probably a good point. *(Looks offstage.)* Here she comes.… I'm not going to tell her now.

DANIEL. No …

ELLEN. I'm not up to it …

DANIEL. Well, we can wait a little while 'till we figure out what to do.

(GLADYS enters.)

GLADYS. What's the matter, Ellen? Ellen? What's the matter?

ELLEN. *(Loud but not too loud:)* I really wish you wouldn't feed the dog scraps. We don't want her to beg.

GLADYS. I want to talk to you about that young — artist — you know — he wants to put up a show —

ELLEN. No he *is* putting up a show.

GLADYS.
But now he says he's leaving!
He's going back to — to where
he lives, and he's leaving me
all his pictures! He says he's
just packing them off and
leaving them there. And —

ELLEN.
What?...No he's not. No he's
not.
DANIEL.
He's just going —
ELLEN.
He's not leaving. Stop talking
a minute. Stop talking.

GLADYS. I never know where he *is*! One day he shows up, one day he's going *away* — I never —

ELLEN. *Listen* to me! He is just going home for the weekend! He will be back on Monday!

GLADYS. Who told you that?

DANIEL and ELLEN. HE DID!

(GLADYS winces in pain and touches her hearing aid.)

GLADYS. What?

DANIEL. *He* did.

ELLEN. He has to go home for a few days to see his mother and to make a little money. He's not leaving you the pictures. He's only going for the weekend.

GLADYS. No.

DANIEL.
Yes! He's going home to make some money and to see his mother.... He wants to see his mother!

ELLEN. *(To DANIEL:)* What are we gonna tell *him*?

GLADYS. Well what's she buggin' him for? *I* can't put up that show myself! I don't know what to do!

DANIEL. You don't have to do anything! He's going to be back in THREE DAYS!

GLADYS. Three days? Why didn't he tell me that?

ELLEN. He did tell you. You just forgot.

GLADYS. I think he's very sneaky.

DANIEL. Fine. He's sneaky. But he'll be back in three days.

ELLEN. *(To DANIEL:)* I'm going to call Arthur. Although I'm sure he'll say there's nothing to be done —

(Offstage the front door opens.)

GLADYS. Has anybody fed the dog?

ELLEN. *(Continued.)* — but I might as well —

(HOWARD comes in, in a suit, carrying a soft briefcase.)

HOWARD. Hello dear. *(Kisses DANIEL.)* How are you?

DANIEL. Hi.

GLADYS. Hello!

HOWARD. *(Kisses GLADYS.)* HELLO GLADYS. *(He crosses away from GLADYS and kisses ELLEN.)* Hello dear.

ELLEN. Mr. George is taking back the gallery.

HOWARD. He's what?

ELLEN. He's building a cafe for the hotel and he wants her to be out in May.

HOWARD. Oh, fuck.

GLADYS . Did anybody feed the dog?

HOWARD. Have you told her?

ELLEN. No, I have to get up my nerve. And I also think I should

call Arthur and see what he thinks —
    HOWARD. Oh, shit.
    GLADYS. *(To DANIEL.)* Honey?
    DANIEL. *(Trying to listen to HOWARD and ELLEN.)* Just a minute ...!

ELLEN.
Although I'm fairly sure there's nothing she can do about it. She doesn't have a lease, I don't think there's anything written down and he wants to put in the cafe *this summer*.
    HOWARD.
When did he call?
    ELLEN.
Ten minutes ago.

GLADYS.
Did anybody give the dog her supper?
    DANIEL.
Not yet. We'll feed her in a few minutes!
    GLADYS.
What?
    DANIEL.
We'll fed her in a few minutes!

GLADYS. Do you think the Village has changed lately?
DANIEL. Yes!
GLADYS. *(Applauds.)* Well! Somebody agrees with me!
DANIEL. Uh huh!

HOWARD.
All right. Why don't you go call Arthur?
    ELLEN.
I don't even know if he's still in the office. He's probably gone by now.

GLADYS.
I sit in that window all day long, and it never used to be so crowded before.
    DANIEL. *(To GLADYS:)*
Uh huh!

HOWARD. Why don't you call him anyway? Call him at home.
ELLEN. I don't want to bother him at home. I can —
HOWARD. Honey —
DANIEL. Mom, for Christ's sake, call him at home. He won't mind.
    HOWARD. Your mother is very pushy.

GLADYS. What's the matter, honey?
DANIEL. Nothing!
ELLEN. Maybe he's still at the office.

(ELLEN exits.)

GLADYS. Where's Ellen going?
DANIEL. Nowhere!
GLADYS. The man who runs that hotel is changing the whole place. I saw him on the street, and his daughter was looking for him and he walked right by her and he wouldn't even talk to her! She was crying. She was. And he's got a lot of people from *Europe* in there now.
DANIEL. Uh huh!
HOWARD. Dan, I was thinking that she likes Daisy so much, it might be a nice thing for her if we got her a little cat.
GLADYS. *(To DANIEL:)* Honey, do you know how to cook?
DANIEL. *(Trying to answer HOWARD:)* A little!
GLADYS. Your mother is a wonderful cook. I never learned how to cook anything!
HOWARD. Dan ...?

DANIEL.	GLADYS.
Yeah, I know, but I told Mom I don't know what she's going to do if she opens the door and it runs out. She couldn't get it back, she can't chase it up the stairs, or if it gets out on the street — *(To GLADYS:)* Yes!	Are you still writing for the newspaper, honey? Honey? Are you still writing for that newspaper?

GLADYS. Are you working hard?
DANIEL. So so!
GLADYS. So so. Well that's good!
HOWARD. Well — it's just a thought. Maybe we could put up a gate ...

(ELLEN enters. During the following, GLADYS hums to herself.)

ELLEN. He's not there. I left him a —

DANIEL. Did you call him at home?

ELLEN. No, I left a message for him at the office. I don't want to bother him at home —

HOWARD. Honey, for Christ's sake!

ELLEN. I will call him in the morning! They're not kicking her out *tomorrow*!

GLADYS. Kicking who out?

(They turn to her, startled that she heard this. Silence.)

ELLEN. Nobody. We're talking about somebody you don't know. *(GLADYS resumes humming.) I* don't know what to tell her. We're going to have to move her in here and then I'm going to slit my wrists.

(GLADYS spots the dog, offstage.)

GLADYS. Look at the dog. She's crying.

DANIEL. No she's not!

GLADYS. She wants to come in here. Nobody's talking to her.

(Pause.)

ELLEN. I'm going to start dinner.

(ELLEN exits.)

END OF ACT I

ACT II

Scene 1

(ELLEN's living room. GLADYS sits on the sofa. ELLEN stands nearby. DANIEL stands downstage, holding an unopened bottle of beer. He addresses the audience:)

DANIEL. Now came the time to tell Gladys they were taking away her gallery. We avoided it for as long as we could because we had no idea what to do with her afterwards. She was starting to lose some words. She couldn't really remember anybody's name except Ellen's, and she didn't recognize anyone outside the immediate family anymore. My father came to New York for a visit and she knew she was glad to see him, but she didn't quite know who he was. Long monologues that used to be part of her regular repertoire dropped out of her conversation for good. I stopped going out to dinner with her because it got to be too much of an ordeal. She rang my doorbell so much, I stopped answering it all the time. Instead, I'd just go to the door and look through the peephole to make sure she was OK, and then I'd watch this weird little convex image of her turn around in the hallway and go back into her apartment.

Every day I came home from work, knowing she'd been alone all afternoon, and I listened at her door, hoping she'd be asleep so I wouldn't have to go in, knowing that if I didn't she'd be alone all night until Marva showed up in the morning.

But as soon as it got warmer she started going to the gallery again. She sat there and talked to Don and anybody else who wandered in, and it really seemed to cheer her up. One time she got hysterical about something when she was alone in the gallery, and the cops came by and this one young cop told me, "She shouldn't be left alone like that: it's not safe." Sometimes people talked as if we weren't facing the true degree of her decline — and maybe we weren't. But I don't know what we were supposed to do. She didn't want to live with Mom any more than Mom wanted to live with her. We never even talked about putting her in a nursing home. She just didn't want to do that. And I thought it was better for her to be at risk alone in the gallery than to be locked in her apartment all day long.

(He opens the beer and goes into the living room to join ELLEN and GLADYS.

[NOTE: While GLADYS now has a lot of trouble finding the right words, she still knows exactly what she is trying to say, and still addresses herself directly to the others with the same dogged persistence and unflagging energy as before. In other words, she is not lost in her own world, or disconnected from the others, or seem as though she is talking to herself. She at all times pressures them for answers, and when they ignore or placate her it drives her even harder to get a response from them.]

GLADYS. I want to sell that — there are two — places, and I want to sell one of them, and find another place. Because I can't *stay* there all day long, and there's a woman there who comes in every day. She's a very good-looking black woman, and I went to the bathroom and she was standing there, standing up, peeing like a man, into the — *cup*.

ELLEN. Have you heard this one yet?

DANIEL. Yeah, you told me.

GLADYS. She was making a pass! And she wouldn't go away! Just *looking* at me! With the door wide open. And the one in the gallery, I told him to go around to the — places, on Madison Avenue, and go in and bring them an — invi — invitation, because he's opening a show —

ELLEN. All right. I'm going to tell her.

DANIEL. All right.

GLADYS. Those pictures have been up for a few weeks now and he hasn't even had the show yet, and I said to him —

ELLEN. LISTEN: MR. GEORGE IS TAKING AWAY THE

GALLERY. HE WANTS TO TAKE THE GALLERY BACK FOR THE HOTEL, SO YOU'RE GOING TO HAVE TO MOVE OUT OF THE GALLERY IN TWO MONTHS, AFTER DON OPENS HIS SHOW.

(Pause.)

GLADYS. Well *good* then. I'll give it up and that'll be that for that, and I'll get a job being a lawyer.

ELLEN. You don't have to worry about that right now. You have another two months before you have to move out, and there's plenty —

GLADYS. Because I can't run that place by myself! So I'll sell it and get myself set up in an — an — a house — an office. *(To DANIEL:)* Maybe you can take that place in the front for me, honey, and you can use it for the newspaper.

DANIEL. No, I don't need another place, that's your apartment. You don't have to move out of your apartment, only the gallery!

GLADYS. As soon as my — foot — gets better, I'm gonna start lookin' around for a town so I can move to another town.

ELLEN. Jesus Christ, she's really — it's word salad.

GLADYS. Because I can't manage by myself! And there's one woman who comes in and sits there — Hm! *(She demonstrates.)* And she doesn't say a word all day long. And I want someone to get *rid* of her.

ELLEN. We can't get rid of her —

GLADYS. They want me to cook for them, and throw a party, and entertain them, but I can't *do* that anymore. I'm sick!

ELLEN. They're there to cook for *you*! They are helping me take care of you, because otherwise I have to come down every day and do your insulin myself. They are there to make things easier for *me*.

GLADYS. Well they *should* help you! You have your own family —

ELLEN. We can talk about that later. I just wanted to tell you that Mr. George is taking back the gallery, but we don't have to do anything for a couple of months!

GLADYS. Well who's gonna take care of all those pictures? I'll have to talk with that man, I know his daughter —

ELLEN. Don will take care of the pictures, he'll take the pictures with him.

GLADYS. Well — I've had that — the — the place —

ELLEN. Gallery.

GLADYS. — gallery, for many years and nobody comes in there. So I'll sell it. You can have the place in the front, and I'll get a job in an office. *(To DANIEL:)* Do they have any jobs in your office, honey?

ELLEN. We can talk about that later. You'll have one last opening with Don's show, and we can worry about your apartment later.

GLADYS. I think that's very sensible. Worry about it later. Good!

(DANIEL and ELLEN look at each other, i.e., it can't be this easy.)

Scene 2

(The gallery. DON's opening. On the desk is a big platter of cheese and crackers, plastic cups and paper napkins, and a big bottle of wine. GLADYS sits behind the desk. DON and DANIEL stand together, across the room from her. Each has a plastic cup of wine. DON is eating cheese. Everyone is in a good mood, especially GLADYS and DON.)

DON. But every time I try to tell her I'm just goin' back home for a few days to see my mother she goes haywire. It's that darn hearing aid.

DANIEL. You've got to be kidding. It's not her hearing aid.

DON. No, I'm tellin' you, it's not a good model. And this stuff about my mother is just plain ridiculous.

DANIEL . Yeah, well, it's been really great that you've been in here, it's been great for her —

GLADYS. Your mother was here before, sweet. I don't know what happened to her. Is she coming down?

DANIEL. She went to do some errands! She'll be back later!

GLADYS.
She came in and then she just went — she — I don't know what happened to her. Do you want some of this — bottle — some of this — Do you want some of this — liquor?

DON.
Yeah, she was in before with your step-father. They came in a few hours ago —

DANIEL.
Yeah, I know, I saw them at the house. *(To GLADYS:)* No thank you! I have some!

DON. Well, I'm really excited. I put an ad in this art news art letter newspaper. I been bustin' my back on these pictures and I don't mind tellin' you I'm pretty excited. You know, I think the problem before was that I didn't really have an "opening." People would look in, but I was workin' on the pictures —

GLADYS. So what's new, honey? Are you working hard? Is everything kablooey in the back of the —

DANIEL. No, everything's fine!

DON. — You know — I was workin' on the pictures literally day and night, and then with the cold weather she didn't come in too much, but now it's all set and the weather's good. I don't know if you noticed the new sign —

DANIEL. Yeah, my cousin Bill made it: he put it up in the winter, didn't he?

DON.
Oh yeah, yeah, right. You been in since then, haven't you?

DANIEL.
Yeah, a lot. I was here when the cops came...

DON.
Yeah, what the heck was that about?

DANIEL.
I don't know. She thought somebody was — *(To GLADYS:)* What?

GLADYS.
I want to sell that place in the — the business in the — When my — toe — I want to get rid of that place, it's too dark for me in the winter. And now there's a little girl —

GLADYS. What's the matter, honey?

DANIEL. NOTHING. I DIDN'T HEAR WHAT YOU SAID.
GLADYS. What did I say?
DANIEL. I don't know.
GLADYS. Well me neither.

(GLADYS laughs. DANIEL laughs too.)

DON. *(Points to a picture.)* I notice a lot of the people who look through the window were payin' attention to this one ...
DANIEL. *(To GLADYS:)* I'M JUST GOING TO LOOK AT THE PICTURES.
GLADYS. Well don't you have to — fix them up in — to get them the way you want it?
DANIEL. UM — NO! I'M GOING TO LOOK AT SOME OF THE PICTURES! THE PAINTINGS!
DON. This is my favorite. That's my mother. You see this macramé over here? She did that by hand, like when I was a kid, and I was always intrigued by that. And one day, she was gonna throw it out —
GLADYS. *(Picks up a piece of cheese.)* Does anybody want some of this — stuff!
DANIEL. NO THANK YOU.
GLADYS. It's delicious!
DON. — And I said, "Why don't you just put it on the wall?" So I put it up for her, made a little frame for it, and then I figured, you know, thread *fades* ...
DANIEL. Uh huh ...
DON. So I figured it's not gonna last forever, so I featured it in the picture. I painted the whole room separately — and then I painted my mother while she was *in* the room. Everything you see is really there in real life. I tried to get the details right, because that's what you remember when you think about something, so I tried like hell to get them the way they are.
DANIEL. It's great ...
GLADYS. Honey? Do you want some? This — cook — cookie is absolutely delicious. Anybody want to try some?
DANIEL. NO THANKS. IN A MINUTE.

(GLADYS starts humming.)

DON. Anyway, I don't know if you like that one ...

DANIEL. Did you — Did you mean to write three thousand dollars? These pictures are three thousand dollars apiece?

DON. No, that one's three thousand, those over there are two, because that's a smaller canvass, and the rest of these are three.

(Pause.)

DANIEL. Gee, I hope you can sell them.

DON. Well, first they gotta come in, right?

(He squints out the picture window.)

DON. That couple's been by about five times now.

DANIEL. I didn't know what time to come by.

DON. Well, we been open for about four and a half, five hours — Since about eleven o'clock this morning. Not too many people came in yet, but it's so beautiful outside today. I tried to get my sister to come in, but it's a big ordeal for her to travel. She's pretty much a stay-at-home. And I don't get on too good with my brother-in-law. He takes good care of her, but he's — I don't know. He's always gotta be tellin' everybody what to do. He's one of those guys.

DANIEL. When I was ten I broke my wrist outside on the hotel awning. Gladys was having a big opening for somebody and I went outside and I was playing tag with some kids, and I whipped around and ran right into the awning pole — and I cracked a bone in my wrist.

DON. Oh yeah?

DANIEL. *(Turning toward the desk.)* And then another time I was in here, and she used to have a coffee maker on the floor by the desk over there, and —

GLADYS. How are you honey?

DANIEL. FINE THANKS.

GLADYS. You havin' a good time? Did you look at the pictures?

DANIEL. YES! I'M LOOKING AT THEM NOW! *(To DON:)* And I kicked over the boiling water and it went all over my leg. Burned the shit out of me. I got all these blisters on my ankle.

DON. Well, I'm pretty excited. I mean I don't usually get too excited, but this whole thing is kind of like a dream come true for me. You know, where I come from, in my town, you tell 'em you paint pictures and they look at you like you got a screw loose or something.

DANIEL. Yeah, it's nice. This was a nice gallery.

DON. Well, you know, Dan — I hope this isn't too presumptuous or anything, but I was thinkin', you know, you must know some of the people in the art department at your newspaper, and I was wondering if it wouldn't be too much trouble to put a bug in their ear and see if they could send somebody down to check out the show.

(Pause.)

DANIEL. Well, um, Don — the thing is, I don't, uh, I don't actually work for a newspaper.

DON. Because even a small blurb can make a big difference to a new show if it's in *The New York Times*. *(Pause.)* What?

DANIEL. I don't work for *The New York Times*.

DON. Oh. Really? What paper do you work for?

DANIEL. No — I don't work for a newspaper. I work for the Environmental Protection Agency....They don't have an art department.

DON.
Didn't I hear Gladys ask you if you were still workin' at *The New York Times?* And you said "Yes!"

DANIEL.
Yeah, I know, I know, but I can't keep telling her —

DANIEL. Don, I — I really don't work for *The New York Times*. I don't even have a subscription.

DON. Oh. Huh. Well. I'm sorry. I — Phooey. Oh well. So you don't know anyone who ... no, huh?

DANIEL. Sorry. I wish I —

GLADYS. Did you look at the pictures, honey?

DANIEL. YEAH, I THINK THEY'RE TERRIFIC.

GLADYS. Would you like me to buy one for you? I think one of these little ones would look just — in your place — in the — do you have pictures up in there?

DANIEL. Yeah, I have a lot!

GLADYS. I've never seen that one. That place in there.

DANIEL. What do you mean? You've seen it a million times!

GLADYS. I've never been in there.

DANIEL. Sure you have. You were in there last week!

GLADYS. Which one do you like, honey? Tell me which — tell me the — the show you like, and I'll fix it up for you. I want to buy it for you.

DANIEL. *(Unsure if he wants a picture)* Well — LET ME LOOK SOME MORE AND I'LL LET YOU KNOW!

GLADYS. Your mother bought two of them —

DANIEL. I KNOW! *(To DON:)* Oh, did she buy another two, or ...

DON. No, no, from when they were in here in the Fall.

DANIEL. Oh yeah, they got 'em for my stepbrother.

DON. Did his wife have the baby?

DANIEL. Yeah, a girl. She had her last month.

DON. I've never been married.

(ELLEN comes in.)

ELLEN. Hello.

DON. Welcome back.

GLADYS. Look, Ellen's here!

ELLEN. *(A joke, to DANIEL and DON:)* Did you recognize me?

DANIEL. Yup.

ELLEN. Any customers?

DON. Not yet, but I think people are really out enjoying the weather today. A lot of people are lookin' in, but I think they'll probably come in more after the weekend.

ELLEN. I'm going to take her home, she must be exhausted.

DON. Yeah, she's been talkin' a mile a minute since we got here this morning.

ELLEN. *(To DANIEL:)* Where's your young lady friend? Didn't you say she might —

DANIEL. Yeah, she had something to do.

ELLEN. Is that situation any better?

DANIEL. Well, yesterday it was.

ELLEN. Oh dear ... not easy.

DANIEL. That's right.

ELLEN. Well, I'm gonna take her home — *(Goes to GLADYS.)* HELLO. WOULD YOU LIKE TO GO HOME?

GLADYS. Sure, are we going to New York?

(ELLEN looks at DANIEL, surprised and distressed by this new cognitive low.)

ELLEN. *(To GLADYS:)* No — We're *in* New York. I said do you want to go home, to your apartment? *(No response. ELLEN looks at DANIEL again, worried, and then back at GLADYS.)* IT'S ALMOST TIME FOR DINNER. WHY DON'T YOU LET ME TAKE YOU HOME?

GLADYS. I had no idea it was so late! Are you tired, honey?

ELLEN. No, it's not late, but it's time to go home!

GLADYS. All right, let me find my purse —

ELLEN. Your purse is on the back of the chair!

GLADYS. Wait — I don't have my keys —

ELLEN. I have your keys, I have them right here,

GLADYS. *(Looks through her bag.)* Wait a minute, let me make sure I've got everything. I don't know where I put my —

(She dumps her purse out on the desk.)

ELLEN. There she goes.

(GLADYS looks through her stuff.)

DANIEL. Mom, I'm gonna go talk to Mr. George.

ELLEN. Well, honey, I already talked to him —

DANIEL. Well let me just try. I'm gonna call him and go see him and see if he can — I mean, she's not gonna be able to —

ELLEN. Well good then, go talk to him. There's certainly nothing to *lose* ...

DANIEL. Yeah, because this is just awful — I mean — I —

DON. What are you gonna try to get him to let us stay open?

DANIEL. Well, I thought I'd go see if I can get another year out of him, because what difference would it make? And she can't —

She's got to have something to do.

ELLEN. *(Sighs.)* Well, good luck.

DANIEL. Yeah, I know, but —

ELLEN. *(To GLADYS.)* WHAT ARE YOU LOOKING FOR? *(Pause.)* WHAT ARE YOU LOOKING FOR?

GLADYS. I'm looking for my keys! I can't find them!

ELLEN. *(Shows keys.)* Your keys are right here! I have them in my hand.

GLADYS. Oh! Where'd you find them?

ELLEN. You gave them to me this morning! COME ON. IT'S TIME TO GO HOME.

(As ELLEN helps GLADYS with her belongings, and helps her up:)

DON. Well, this is just great. I want to thank all of you, because this has been just tremendous for me. I know things are gonna work out now for me, because I really believe that if you want something bad enough you can have it as long as you don't quit trying. I mean — Greenwich Village — New York City gallery. I've been waiting for this day my whole life.

Scene 3

(ELLEN's living room. GLADYS sits in a rocker. ELLEN sits on the sofa looking through a mail-order catalogue. DANIEL and HOWARD stand apart.)

DANIEL. It was *the* most depressing thing I ever saw. Nobody comes in all day long, she's behind the desk — oblivious, like she's hosting a party, and he's standing around eating cheese in this empty gallery and he says to us, "I've been waiting for this day *my whole life.*" It was just —

HOWARD. Jesus Christ.

DANIEL. It was the most depressing thing I ever saw —

HOWARD. Jesus Christ. That *is* really depressing … Oy. I'm

gonna call my folks. *(Takes a step.)* Dan, I called my folks last night and my mother picked up, and she was very upset, crying — and she said, "I can't stand it any more, he's terrible, he's driving me crazy, he won't listen to anybody, he's so awful ..." So I said "Listen, he's ninety-three years old. He's a little difficult. Put him on the phone." He gets on the phone, I say "Listen, Dad, what's the matter? Mom seems very upset." He says "*I'll* tell you what's the matter — I knew this marriage was a mistake sixty-three years ago. I'm leaving, I'm getting a divorce, and I'm moving to China." So what do you think of that?

DANIEL. Wow.

HOWARD. *(Moving to exit.)* So things are good all over with the old folks, right? If you don't lose your marbles and one of you doesn't die young you get old together and torture each other to death.

DANIEL. Great.

HOWARD. See if I can calm him down ... So fucking crazy ...

(He exits. GLADYS looks at the dog, offstage.)

GLADYS. Look at the dog. Ellen. Look at the dog. She's showing off. Isn't that sweet? That is the sweetest little animal. Look, she knows we're talking about her. She's showing off.

DANIEL. She doesn't know we're talking about her, she's a dog!

GLADYS. I had a beautiful little dog. Did you ever meet my dog, honey?

DANIEL. Sure!

GLADYS. Do you remember her?

DANIEL. Of course I remember her.

GLADYS. What?

DANIEL. I said I REMEMBER HER.

GLADYS. You do? She was the sweetest little thing. Ellen, do you remember that little dog I had?

(ELLEN doesn't answer. She turns the page of her catalogue.)

GLADYS. This one is a little devil. Always sniffin' around somewhere. Look, she has a — a paw. She's scared you're gonna put her out in the street. She's trying to sing to you. Look at her. Don't you think I should give her something?

ELLEN. NO!

GLADYS. All right. *(To DANIEL:)* Do you know how to cook?

DANIEL. *(Sighs.)* A little bit.

GLADYS. You do! That's wonderful. I never cooked much. In that place, I have a little — fire, and I make myself a little sandwich. Does Ellen like to cook?

(ELLEN puts down the catalogue.)

GLADYS. Ellen? Do you know how to cook?

(Pause. ELLEN is really shocked.)

ELLEN. I've been cooking you dinner here every Wednesday for twenty years.

GLADYS. *(Laughs.)* Well where did you learn how to fix it up? Who told you?

ELLEN. I think she's gotten worse.

DANIEL. Oh, Mom.

GLADYS. You know, that one — the one in the back — he says he's leaving because his mother doesn't want him to be here —

ELLEN: *(On "want":)* No, it's got nothing to do with his mother —

GLADYS. What?

ELLEN. He's leaving because the hotel is taking back the gallery!

GLADYS. Yes, I know that ...

ELLEN. He has to go back because he doesn't have a job and you have to get out of the gallery.

GLADYS. Well, what am I going to *do* all day long? *(Silence.)* I can't stay cooped up in that place all day long by myself! I'll go crazy.

ELLEN. We can talk about that later.

GLADYS. I think I'm going to look around and set myself up in a … in a … in a ...

ELLEN. See? She forgets a lot of words ...

GLADYS. In a little — you know, maybe I can get some work as a lawyer in an office. I still have a — paper — a — passport — and I can do a little of it — I don't need much, but I have to get out and do *some*thing —

ELLEN. Let's just get the gallery settled first and then we can worry about that later.

GLADYS. I think I'll go talk to that one who runs the — the hotel. I know his daughter —

ELLEN. There's nothing to talk to him about — *(To DANIEL:)* By the way, did you ever call Mr. George? Or did you decide —

DANIEL. Yeah, no, I'm gonna try to go see him this week, but I don't know if it'll do any —

GLADYS. What?

ELLEN. There is nothing to talk to him about —

DANIEL. THERE'S PROBABLY NOTHING WE CAN DO. YOU DON'T HAVE A LEASE.

GLADYS. Well maybe you and I can set something up in that place in the back. Would you like that honey?

DANIEL. Let's worry about one thing at a time!

GLADYS. One thing at a time. You know, I think that's very smart. We'll do it one — word — at a time.

DANIEL. Good!

GLADYS. Good. *(Pause.)* Look at the dog … ohhhhh, look at the poor thing, she's hungry — I'm gonna give her just a little something —

(GLADYS picks up a plate of crackers.)

ELLEN. DON'T *FEED* HER! SHE'S ALREADY EATEN! She's getting too FAT! DON'T FEED HER!!!

GLADYS. Well why are you so angry?

(ELLEN gets up and grabs the plate.)

ELLEN. I'VE TOLD YOU *TEN THOUSAND TIMES* NOT TO FEED HER! SHE'S TOO FAT AND SHE'S ALREADY EATEN!

DANIEL. Mom! She can't help it!

ELLEN. *(Starts to cry.)* Well I can't help it either, I can't *stand* it!

(ELLEN runs into the other room.)

GLADYS. *(Bursts into tears.)* Why is she angry at me? What did I do?

DANIEL. She's not angry, she's just tired. She doesn't want you to feed the dog.

GLADYS. Well I'm not going to stay here if nobody wants me, I'll go home! *(Still crying, she gets up with great difficulty.)* I don't know why she's always so angry at me! What did I do? Why is she yelling at me? I don't understand!

DANIEL. *(Calling:)* Mom ...!

GLADYS. I'm going home, I'm going to kill myself.

DANIEL. DON'T KILL YOURSELF.

GLADYS. *(Looks for her purse.)* Well I can't stay cooped up in that apartment all day long! No one ever comes in there!

DANIEL. PLEASE SIT DOWN. IT'S ALL RIGHT, WE'LL FIND YOU SOMETHING ELSE TO DO —

GLADYS. I can't stand it in there and I don't want to come here if nobody wants me here. I'll go home and kill myself. Where's my purse? I lost my purse!

DANIEL. IT'S ON THE ARM OF YOUR CHAIR —

GLADYS. Why is Ellen so angry at me?

(ELLEN comes back in and stands there.)

DANIEL. Will you tell her you're not mad at her?!

GLADYS. I can't find my keys! I lost my keys! I won't be able to get back in! What am I going to do? I won't have anywhere to sleep! I'll be sleeping on the street!

ELLEN. *(Comes forward, softly:)* Your keys are in your bag. But you don't have to leave. Do you want some coffee?

GLADYS. I don't want to stay if you're going to yell at me! I don't know what I did!

ELLEN. I'm not yelling at you, everything's fine.

(HOWARD enters.)

GLADYS. I want to get another — place — He won't take the

pictures down, he says he's going *home*!

(The doorbell rings.)

GLADYS.	ELLEN.
And if he leaves the pictures up I can't *do* it by myself — I don't understand. What's the matter?	Hold on a minute, sit down, I have to get the door. Howard, will you get the *door*?
	DANIEL.
	I'll get it.

ELLEN. I have to get the doorbell. Just wait one second!

GLADYS.	DANIEL. *(Going:)*
I can't find my money —	Mom, I'm *getting* it!

ELLEN. You don't need any money. That's Don and he's going to take you home in a taxi.

GLADYS. Does he know the way?

ELLEN. Yes, he knows the way —

GLADYS. But I haven't got my keys!

ELLEN. *(Looking through GLADYS' bag.)* I'm just finding them, they're in your bag.

HOWARD. ELLEN IS FINDING THEM!

(DANIEL brings DON in.)

DANIEL. Hi, we're having a little scene here.

DON. Oh, that's all right.

GLADYS. I don't understand anything. I can't go home without my keys!

ELLEN. *(Waving the keys.)* Here they are. They're right here. Don't cry. Your keys are right here. Stop crying.

(The keys are on an elastic bracelet. ELLEN puts them on GLADYS' wrist.)

GLADYS. What?

ELLEN. There's nothing to cry about.

GLADYS. What's wrong with crying?

HOWARD. NOTHING.

ELLEN.
Sit down and take your time.
Look, Don's here now, and
he's going to take you home
in a taxi. I'll call you in the
morning when you're feel-
ing better.
GLADYS.
I can't breathe.

HOWARD. *(To DON:)*
Hello.
DON.
Hi there.
HOWARD.
Just another evening at the Fine
house.
DON.
Yeah ...

ELLEN. Because you're in a panic.

GLADYS. I am in a panic. I can't breathe ... I'm dizzy ...

ELLEN. Just sit down. Nothing's wrong with you, you're just upset.

GLADYS. *(Sitting.)* All right, I'll sit down.

(She bursts into tears again.)

ELLEN. Come on, don't cry ...

GLADYS. *(Getting up again.)* I don't want to go out on the street!

ELLEN. Nobody's going on the street. You're going to settle down and then Don is going to take you home in a taxi and I'll talk to you tomorrow.

GLADYS. Where's my bag?

ELLEN. It's right here.

GLADYS.
I had a coat when I came in.
ELLEN.
No you didn't. It's very
warm out. You didn't bring
a coat.
GLADYS.
I didn't?
ELLEN.
No.

HOWARD. *(To DON:)*
Was the traffic bad coming up?
Did you take a taxi, or did you
drive your car?
DON.
No, I took a taxi because you
can't get a parking space down
there if you wait too late ...
HOWARD.
All right. We'll refund you.

GLADYS.
Well now I upset you.

DON.
Oh, that's all right. You don't have to --

ELLEN.
I'm not upset. You are.

HOWARD.
Don't be ridiculous. We'll pay for it.

GLADYS.
Yes. I am upset. I'm sorry honey. I'm all mixed up.

DON.
Well, uh ...

ELLEN.
It's all right.

GLADYS. *(To DON:)* Hello. We're having a — *(Makes a fist.)* a punch-up. *(She laughs.)*

ELLEN. "Ha ha ha."

DON. Hello, Gladys!

GLADYS. What did he say?

ELLEN. He said hello. Now, do you have everything?

GLADYS. Yes. Where are my keys?

ELLEN. Around your wrist.

GLADYS. *(Rattling them.)* Oh here they are. *(Laughs.)* They're right here.

(Silence.)

GLADYS. What's everyone so upset about?

HOWARD. WE'RE UPSET BECAUSE IT'S A SHAME ABOUT THE GALLERY.

GLADYS. We'll I'm upset too!

HOWARD. IT WAS A WONDERFUL PLACE FOR YOU BUT IT'S BEEN VERY DIFFICULT FOR YOU TO MANAGE LATELY!

ELLEN. Don't shout, Howard.

HOWARD. BUT IT WAS A WONDERFUL PLACE AND YOU HAD A LOT OF GOOD YEARS THERE.

GLADYS. Yes I did.

HOWARD. LISTEN, IT'S NO FUN TO GET OLD.

GLADYS. What?

HOWARD. I SAID IT'S NO FUN GETTING OLD!

GLADYS. Well why do you always say that to me? Nobody wants to hear that — !

HOWARD. *(Surprised.)* I'M SORRY. I GUESS I'M NOT SO TACTFUL. I won't say it anymore.

GLADYS. "You're old! You're getting old!" That's not a helpful thing to say.

HOWARD. I — I'm sorry. Sometimes I'm not so smart.

GLADYS. Sure you're smart! This whole family's smart! *(To DON:)* Do you have money for a taxi?

DON. Yep, right here.

GLADYS. I'm very angry at you.

DON. I just got here.

HOWARD. That doesn't matter!

DANIEL. *(Kissing her.)* Bye, Grandma.

GLADYS. Good bye, honey. When will I see you?

DANIEL. I'll see you tomorrow.

GLADYS. Do you want a ride with us? Are you going to the city?

DANIEL. No — We're in the city. I'm going home on my bicycle.

GLADYS. But if you came with us you could ride in a taxicab.

DANIEL. I want to take my bike, I like riding it!

GLADYS. All right. *(To ELLEN:)* He says he wants to ride his bicycle.

ELLEN. Yes, I heard him. I'm standing right here. *(Kisses GLADYS.)*

GLADYS. Goodbye honey.

ELLEN. I'll call you tomorrow.

GLADYS. *(To DON:)* What are *you* upset about?

DON. I'm not upset.

HOWARD. Gladys, *you're* upset!

GLADYS. I am upset. I'm all — mixed up. *(She starts to cry again.)* I don't want to stay in that place with those women! They don't talk to you and I don't know what to say to them! They sit there all day long and they never say two words to anybody!

ELLEN. We can talk about it tomorrow.

GLADYS. I don't understand what happened. Herb and I had a *good* life! We had a good life ...!

HOWARD. Yes you did.
GLADYS. I don't understand what happened to me ...
ELLEN. Don't cry. We'll figure something out tomorrow.
GLADYS. Tomorrow. All right. I'm very upset.

(GLADYS and DON go out.)

HOWARD. Good night, Don.
DON. *(Off.)* So long ...

(ELLEN closes the door. Pause.)

ELLEN. I know everybody has to get *old* ...

(She stops talking. They all stand by the door for a moment.)

Scene 4

(DANIEL comes forward.)

DANIEL. *(To the audience:)* I did go to see Mr. George. I asked him for another year. Just one more year before he took away the gallery, because after that it wouldn't make any difference anymore. And I thought it would make a great difference now.

He was very sympathetic. He said he had an aunt who was going through the same thing. But he told me the same thing he told my mother on the phone. The cafe was scheduled to open *that* summer, and there was absolutely nothing he could do about it.

Then he asked if we'd given any thought to putting Gladys in a home. I got kind of angry and I said we didn't really want to do that. She didn't like old people. She liked to be where the action was. She thought she was running a gallery. He said this is really the time her family should be taking care of her. And that was the end of that.

I kept thinking there must be something we could do, only I just couldn't think of what it was. I had a dream where I put her on a bus from Vermont to New York, and I wanted to get her settled and get off, but as she hobbled down the aisle I was afraid she'd be knocked over by the bus's motion, and it occurred to me that she'd never know where to change buses, that it was impossible to put her on a bus by herself because she'd never make it. But I couldn't go with her, and it was all too late. Her mind was smashed to pieces, and the person she used to be hadn't really been around for a long time. But the pieces were still *her* pieces. *(Pause.)* I guess we all wanted to get out of it.

(As a clock chimes twelve, the LIGHTS RISE on the hallway between GLADYS' and DANIEL's apartments. GLADYS, wearing an old housecoat, comes out of her apartment, crosses very slowly to DANIEL's front door and rings the bell, a loud, horrible electric buzzer of a doorbell. Pause. She rings it again. Pause. She turns around and starts to walk slowly back to her door. DANIEL, half asleep, opens his door, putting on a bathrobe.)

DANIEL. HELLO ...!

GLADYS. *(Turning:)* Hello? Hello?

DANIEL. HELLO. WHAT'S THE MATTER?

GLADYS. Ohhhhh, I'm sorry sweetie, did I wake you?

DANIEL. YES!

GLADYS. Ohhhhh, I'm sorry. I tried to ring your doorbell yesterday and nobody was there. I didn't know where you were. I was worried. You weren't home.

DANIEL. So *what*?

GLADYS.
Well I didn't know where you were. Where is your mother? I tried to call her but she's not home.

DANIEL.
I'm here *now* — and Mom is asleep — You probably —

GLADYS. What, honey?

DANIEL. *(Slowly and distinctly.)* You probably misdialed. Mom is probably asleep. It's after midnight!

GLADYS. Oh, do you want to come in and sit down?

DANIEL. NO. I WANT TO GO BACK TO SLEEP. IT'S VERY LATE.

GLADYS. Oh. All right. I'm awfully sorry I woke you, honey.

DANIEL. That's OK.

GLADYS. Are you like me? Can you go right back to sleep?

DANIEL. YES.

GLADYS. All right honey, I'm sorry.

DANIEL. IT'S ALL RIGHT.

(He goes back inside. She goes very slowly inside her apartment. Muffled and distant, we hear the church bells chime three o'clock. GLADYS comes back out, fully dressed, carrying her purse. She crosses very slowly to DANIEL's front door and rings the bell. Pause. She rings again. DANIEL jerks open the door, hair rumpled, in his underwear.)

GLADYS. What's the matter, honey, is the house burning down?

DANIEL. What?

GLADYS. Is the house burning down?

DANIEL. No!

GLADYS. Where did your mother go, honey? Is she in your apartment?

DANIEL. No!

GLADYS.
Well why didn't she say goodbye to me! She was here before and then she ran out and she didn't say goodbye! I don't know where she went! Why did she leave like that? What did I do to her?

DANIEL.
What? Mom wasn't here!

No — No — Listen a — Listen a minute.

DANIEL. She hasn't been here for hours! She was here last night — LAST NIGHT!

GLADYS. But why didn't she say goodbye?!

DANIEL. She *did* say goodbye. She said goodbye last night! And now it's after midnight and she's home asleep!

GLADYS. No!

DANIEL. YES! SHE WAS HERE BEFORE AND SHE SAID GOODBYE AND NOW IT'S AFTER MIDNIGHT!

GLADYS. Well why did she run out like that? I thought we were going to the country!

DANIEL. NO! YOU'RE MIXED UP! NOBODY'S GOING TO THE COUNTRY!

GLADYS. *They* don't have to invite me! I'll just stay here by myself!

DANIEL. THEY'RE NOT IN THE COUNTRY!

GLADYS. But where are they?

DANIEL. AT HOME IN BED!

GLADYS. Why? What time is it?

DANIEL. IT IS THREE O'CLOCK IN THE MORNING!

GLADYS. *(Hand to mouth, shocked.)* I had no idea it was so late.

DANIEL. WELL IT IS.

GLADYS. *(Bursts into tears.)* But why didn't your mother tell me she was leaving!

DANIEL. SHE *DID* TELL YOU! SHE *DID* TELL YOU!

GLADYS. NO! SHE NEVER TOLD ME ANYTHING — !

DANIEL. YES SHE *DID*!

GLADYS. NO!

DANIEL. YOU NEVER BELIEVE *ANY*BODY!

GLADYS. BUT SHE NEVER TOLD ME SHE WAS LEAVING!

(DANIEL actually slams his own head into his front door. GLADYS gasps and takes a step back.)

DANIEL. MOM IS ASLEEP! HOWARD IS ASLEEP! IT IS THREE O'CLOCK IN THE MORNING! *(Pause. Slightly calmer:)* THEY WERE HERE LAST NIGHT. THEY SAID GOODBYE, AND YOU'RE GOING UP THERE FOR DINNER ON WEDNESDAY!

GLADYS. You're very angry.

DANIEL. No, but I'M TRYING TO GET SOME SLEEP!

GLADYS. What's the matter honey? Are you having trouble sleeping? *(DANIEL starts to answer. He half-laughs.)* I thought Ellen was mad at me.

DANIEL. NO. NOBODY'S MAD AT ANYBODY.

GLADYS. Well that's all I care about. Do you want to come inside for a minute?

DANIEL. NO, I WANT TO GO BACK TO SLEEP. IT'S VERY LATE AT NIGHT. YOU SHOULD TRY TO SLEEP ALSO! AND I'LL SEE YOU LATER.

GLADYS. All right, honey. I'm sorry.

DANIEL. It's all right!

(GLADYS turns around and walks slowly to her door. DANIEL turns and goes inside his apartment as she goes inside hers. Pause. The distant clock chimes five.)

GLADYS. *(Off.)* Help! Help! Somebody help me! *(GLADYS comes out from her apartment.)* Help! Help! Somebody stole my dog! Help! Help! *(DANIEL opens his door and runs out, tying his bathrobe around him.)* Honey help me, somebody stole my dog! They ran out into the street and —

DANIEL. Grandma —

GLADYS. — I can't find her anywhere! I think somebody stole her!

DANIEL. Grandma you don't have a dog —

GLADYS. What are you talking about! She's gone!

DANIEL. Nobody stole your dog. She died a long time ago. You're having a bad dream.

GLADYS. But they were just in here —

DANIEL. Who was in here?

GLADYS.
Billy and Pearl — They were in here two minutes ago and they ran out, and the dog ran out, and I can't *find* her!

DANIEL
No! Listen to me --

PLEASE LISTEN TO ME!

GLADYS. I'm listening.

DANIEL. You are having a dream. The dog died many years ago. Billy and Pearl are in Fairfield, in Connecticut. They've been there for fifteen years, they weren't here. You've been having a bad dream.

GLADYS. Do you want to go upstairs and check?

DANIEL. No. It's five o'clock in the morning, nobody is here but you and me, there's no dog. There is no dog.

GLADYS. Are you sure?

DANIEL. Yes.

GLADYS. *(Doubtful:)* Well, all right ...

DANIEL. Come into your apartment. Did you eat anything yesterday? *(He takes her into her apartment as they talk. The lights go up in her living room.)* Sometimes when you don't eat you get a little confused. I want you to eat something —

GLADYS. But I'm not hungry. I have to fix something for the people to eat for dinner — I can't —

DANIEL. No, nobody is coming for dinner. It's very early in the morning and I want you to eat something. Sit down here. Sit down. SIT DOWN.

GLADYS. But they'll be looking for me — !

DANIEL. NO! NOBODY'S LOOKING FOR YOU! SIT DOWN!

(She sits in a chair. He exits.)

GLADYS. Maybe you should check upstairs. I think something happened to them. There were — three of them, and they came in and they —— *(She stares at the empty chair.)* Where — *(DANIEL enters with a bowl of yogurt. He puts it in front of her.)* Is he going to get coffee? Oh, no I couldn't eat anything, I'm not hungry!

DANIEL. Just eat this — please!

GLADYS. But I'm not hungry!

DANIEL. IF YOU DON'T EAT THIS I'M GOING TO KILL MYSELF!

GLADYS. But I *can't* — !

DANIEL. PLEASE PLEASE PLEASE PLEASE PLEASE PLEASE EAT THIS! *PLEASE*!

(He's screaming so much she starts eating.)

GLADYS. This is delicious.

DANIEL. Good.

GLADYS. It's very good. *(She eats.)* So what's new with you, honey? Are you working hard? *(DANIEL laughs.)*

GLADYS. Are you still working for the — the television?

DANIEL. Yes!

GLADYS. For the magazine? And people call you and you bring them here and fix up what you want them to do for you?

DANIEL. Yes.

GLADYS. What are you doing now?

DANIEL. Um, I'm —

GLADYS. *(Twists around.)* Where did he go?

(Pause.)

DANIEL. Who?

GLADYS. *(Points at an empty chair.)* Didn't you see him?

DANIEL. *(Very rattled:)* Who? There's nobody there.

GLADYS. He was sitting right there, just a minute ago. Your — Herb! Your *brother*. Where did he go?

(Pause.)

DANIEL. He — he's not here.

GLADYS. What?

(DANIEL looks at her for a long moment.)

DANIEL. He'll be back later.

GLADYS. Do you want me to give him a message for you?

DANIEL. Um —

(GLADYS voice has now dropped to a normal level we haven't heard before. She seems calmer and more self-possessed, more like her old self must have been once. She seems to have momentarily

crossed over to another place altogether. She speaks as if DAN-IEL is just one of three or four people in the room with whom she is talking.)

GLADYS. I used to work for Herb in that lab, you know, when Herb and I were living in Germany. We used to play tennis and go dancing — and it was really rather nice. But that was when the Nazis were marchin' around all over the place, so after a while we decided to get the hell out of there and come home.

DANIEL. Can you understand me?

(GLADYS looks right at him, but it's impossible to tell who or what she is really seeing or hearing.)

GLADYS. What?

DANIEL. Can you understand what I'm saying?

GLADYS. I don't know. I never knew what I was doing! *(D A N - IEL gets up and goes to the phone. GLADYS does not notice. She turns to someone else and keeps going:)* But when we got to that train station, they were all there to stamp your ticket, and he takes my ticket and he looks at me and he says, "Bist du judische?" Do you know what that means? It means "Are you Jewish?" And I looked at him and I said, "Ich spreche kein Deutsche — I don't speak German." *(Pause.)* But when I took Ellen down South to visit Herb at the army base, it was so damn hot down there, all you could do is sit on the porch and fan yourself! There was no one to talk to. Everyone needs someone to talk to, otherwise you'd just go nutty. I love to talk to people. *(DANIEL dials the phone.)* I'm havin' a good time! *(DANIEL starts crying suddenly and keeps dialing.)* Everybody likes to have a good time. What's wrong with that? *(She eats.)*

DANIEL.
Mom. Hi, it's me, I'm sorry to wake you — Well I don't know. She's completely out of her mind. She's hallucinating I don't know what, and she's

GLADYS.
We never did what anybody told us! We used to sneak out of the house all the time! We'd go up to Harlem to hear music, we'd

DANIEL. *(Continued.)* literally talking nonstop. I haven't slept in three days, she wakes me five times a night, and she never, never stops ringing my doorbell and I can't take it anymore. I'm really sorry. *(He starts crying again.)* Can you come get her? O.K. Yeah. All right. I'm really sorry. *(He hangs up.)*

GLADYS. *(Continued.)* go out dancing…. We had a marvelous time. We really did. Now I used to play a lot of tennis, but I was never very good at it. I just played for the fun of it. You know. But Jean was a wonderful tennis player, oh, she was marvelous. And you know Ellen was a wonderful tennis player when she was a teenager. Oh, everybody likes to do those things. Nobody likes sittin' around in a stuffy old house with a lot of boring people. You know?

(DANIEL sits on the sofa.)

GLADYS. But Ellen's always been shy, poor thing. We were so happy when she married Mark because he's had a rough time, he really has. You can't spend all your time running around, nobody'll know what you're talking about! *(DANIEL shuts his eyes.)* But Mark is very charming, he works very hard, he's a hell of a nice guy, and he's a damn good doctor. *(To DANIEL:)* You're a good doctor.

(The Lights FADE OUT. The distant clock chimes eight times.)

Scene 5

(The lights COME UP on DANIEL, asleep on the sofa. GLADYS is offstage. We can just hear her talking steadily in her sleep.)

GLADYS. *(Murmurs offstage:)* … There were the four of us. My sisters were Harriet and Jean, and there was Harold, of course. He was the youngest. And we had a big old house out in Brooklyn. Of course this was a long time ago ...

(ELLEN uses her key to come into the apartment. DANIEL wakes up with a start.)

ELLEN. Hello.

DANIEL . Oh — Hi.

ELLEN. Did you get any sleep?

DANIEL. Not really. I was afraid she would wander outside.... She finally went to sleep an hour ago....Except she's been talking in her sleep non-stop....Man, she sure does like to talk.

ELLEN. Oh dear. I'm sorry Danny. I feel just terrible. We'll take her for a few days and let you get some sleep.

DANIEL. *(Yawning.)* Yeah, I could really use it ...

ELLEN. I really think we're going to have to move her in with us after the summer. She can't stay here anymore. And if we can rent this place out as an office, we could get a couple of thousand bucks for it and use the money to hire somebody around the clock, because this is really no good ...Anyway, why don't you go in your apartment and get some sleep.

DANIEL. Yeah, alright.

(Pause.)

ELLEN. How are things with you and that girl? You said she ...

DANIEL. Um, yeah, she started dating one of my friends.

ELLEN. Oh dear.

DANIEL. She says that my feelings for her are not her issue.

ELLEN. Not her what?

DANIEL . I don't know. I don't really want to talk about it.

ELLEN. OK ...

DANIEL. I guess I'll give her one more try and then give up.

GLADYS. *(Murmurs offstage :)* ... We were very lucky. Our parents gave us a wonderful education....We went to museums and concerts and galleries.... I never liked school very much, I was always sneakin' off to the library to read plays ...

(She trails off.)

DANIEL. She spent the whole night talking about Herb and Harold and her sisters ...

ELLEN. It's all *in* there, I guess. It's just ... it's just all — jumbled up.... *(Pause.)* I *wish* — she would just die peacefully in her sleep, but Dr. Wagner says there's nothing wrong with her physically. She could go on like this for another ten years ...

DANIEL. Great.

GLADYS. *(Murmurs offstage:)* ... Well, we were very anxious naturally, because nobody ever explained it to us and we just didn't know what to do ...

ELLEN. I wonder what she *thinks*. If she thinks anything.

DANIEL. I don't know ...

ELLEN. Well ... when I get senile just put a bullet through my head.

(There is a startled pause.)

DANIEL. You won't get senile.

(Silence. DON lets himself into the apartment with a key.)

DON. Oh — Good morning.

ELLEN. Good morning.

DON. Anything the matter?

ELLEN. No, nothing. She had a bad night, so I'm gonna take her uptown for a few days ...

DON. Oh. Oh.

ELLEN. How are you?

DON. Uh ... well, not so good to tell you the honest truth — uh —

ELLEN. Why? What's the m —

DON. — somebody smashed the windows in my car last night.

ELLEN and DANIEL. What?

DON.
Somebody smashed all
my windows --

DANIEL.
What is going *on*?
    ELLEN. *(With DANIEL:)*
I *saw* a bunch of windows
smashed up —

DON. Yeah! I just went to move my car and three of the windows were smashed in. I asked the doorman in front of the building on the corner if he saw what happened and he said the night guy told him some kids came by last night in a limousine or somethin' and —

ELLEN. Oh my God ...

DON. And one of 'em jumped out of the car and — You want to get this? He smashed in the windows of a buncha cars with one of those — with a giant-sized bottle of champagne.

ELLEN. Are you serious?

DON. Yeah! The guy just went up and down the street smashin' in windows, jumps back in the limousine and drives away down the street.

DANIEL. Jesus Christ.

DON. Do you believe that? I mean, what the hell is *that*?

ELLEN. Did anybody *see* them?

DON. Yeah somebody saw 'em, the night doorman saw the whole thing! He's the one who told the day guy about it. And I asked him, I said "Why the heck didn't the guy *do* something? What, the guy just stands there and watches 'em breakin' everybody's windows?"

DANIEL. Those cars get smashed all the time.

DON. I don't even know if I'm covered for vandalism. I know I'm covered for theft ... I ... You know, Ellen, I don't want to let you down or anything, but I guess I've had it. I'm pretty optimistic by nature, but I gotta admit I'm very, very discouraged by this city. I mean, I surrender. You know? I gotta go home. I can't — I can't even afford this. You been great to me, but ...

(Silence.)

ELLEN. I wouldn't think you could *break* a car window with a bottle.

DON. I guess those giant-sized bottles are made of pretty thick glass. Who knows? Anyway, I figured I'd tell Gladys I can't go to the gallery today. Cops said I should come in and file a report, but what the hell are *they* gonna do? I mean, they should talk to the friggin' night doorman, is what they should do. But ...

(Pause.)

ELLEN . Well — you have keys to the gallery, right? So ...

DON. Yeah, I'll pack the stuff up tomorrow morning. I might have to make two trips but I'll let you know what I'm gonna do. Hope nobody hikes the car while it's sittin' there with no windows. I, uh — I'm feeling very depressed.

ELLEN. Well, I'm sorry. That's very unpleasant.

DANIEL. Yeah ...

DON. I'll say it's unpleasant. *(Pause.)* All right, so ... where's she gonna be, your house?

ELLEN. Yeah, for a few days at least, if you want to —

DON. OK, I'll swing by later and say goodbye to her, probably tomorrow.... I'd sure like to get my hands on whoever it was.... I don't know if they were white or black or what, but ... they probably were *white*. I was always worried about these crazy drug guys. Just goes to show you ...

ELLEN. Well — That is really revolting.

DON. Well — *I* don't live here.

ELLEN. OK, Don, see you later.

DANIEL. So long.

DON. Yeah so long.

(DON exits.)

ELLEN. That is really charming ...

GLADYS. *(Off.)* Ohhhhhh! Ellen? Ellen? Where's Ellen? *(They listen closely, thinking she's awake. Pause. Off, still asleep.)* I don't know when they're going to get there.... We never did it that way before ...

(ELLEN heads into GLADYS' bedroom.)

Scene 6

(DANIEL comes forward. Behind him, HOWARD enters, carrying boxes. Under DANIEL's speech, ELLEN enters with GLADYS, who is dressed in a coat. She sits her down and puts her sneakers on for her as HOWARD moves boxes. They are moving GLADYS out.)

DANIEL. *(To the audience:)* After the summer was over, Mom and Howard moved Gladys out of her apartment and up to their building. When I went by the hotel in the fall, I saw that Mr. George had not yet begun construction in the gallery. It was exactly as Gladys had left it when we moved her out. Even her desk was still there.... A year and a half later, he still hadn't begun construction, and when he finally did, the restaurant didn't actually open until two summers had gone by. And it wasn't a breakfast cafe, it was just a regular restaurant. It wasn't even attached to the rest of the hotel.

(Pause. It seems like he has more to say, but he just stands there for a moment.)

HOWARD. Dan.

DANIEL. *(Turns.)* Yeah ...

HOWARD. *Can you give me a hand with door, dear? (DANIEL opens the door for HOWARD, who goes out carrying a box.)* Thank you.

ELLEN. *(To GLADYS:)* OK, WE'RE GOING TO GO NOW.

GLADYS. Are we going to New York?

ELLEN. Yes. Come on. It's time to go.

GLADYS. Who's gonna keep an eye on the — Honey, who's gonna keep an eye on the basement?

ELLEN. WE'LL TAKE CARE OF THE APARTMENT. YOU DON'T HAVE TO WORRY ABOUT THAT ANYMORE.

GLADYS. Well he's worried because he doesn't have a place to stay in the summer time! Are you going to go back for the summer?

ELLEN. NO, IT'S OCTOBER NOW. WE'RE NOT GOING ANYWHERE.

GLADYS. There are two — places in the back. Have you seen
those little places? I want to get out when the weather gets better and
find myself a little job, because —

ELLEN. COME ON OUT TO THE CAR.

GLADYS. What's the matter? Where am I going?

ELLEN. We're all going uptown together!

GLADYS. *(Beginning to panic.)* But where are you taking me? I
can't go outside, I don't have any money!

ELLEN. You don't need any money. Howard and I are going uptown to MY house in the CAR.

GLADYS.	ELLEN.
No! I don't want to go! Why	It's all right, it's time to —
are you throwing me out?	

ELLEN. We're not throwing you out, we're all going together.

GLADYS. *(Crying.)* But I don't want to go anywhere, I want to
go to New York, I want to get a job!

ELLEN. *(Walking her toward the door.)* We are going to New
York! We're all going there now and we're going to have some dinner!

GLADYS. I don't *want* to go outside — I don't have any —
shoulder — I don't have any *weapons* — Why are you trying to kill
me?

ELLEN. Nobody is killing you. Howard will take you out to the
car and I'll be right there and then we're going for a short trip in the
car to my house, and we'll all be together the whole time. The car is
right outside.

GLADYS. Are you going to Brooklyn? Is everybody going to
Brooklyn?

HOWARD. *(Gently takes her arm.)* WE'RE GOING UPTOWN
TO OUR HOUSE. IT'S A VERY SHORT TRIP.

GLADYS. *(Crying again.)* I don't want to go, I don't understand
where you're taking me! I don't want to go by myself!

HOWARD. We'll be with you the whole time. Keep walking.

GLADYS. Keep walking. I don't even know where I'm going!
What did I ever do to you?

HOWARD. You didn't do anything and nothing bad is going to happen.

GLADYS. I don't want to go! Where's Ellen? I don't understand why I have to go! I want to paint that place and sell it to the real estate and nobody ever *listens to me*! Wait — wait — I don't have my keys!

HOWARD. YOUR KEYS ARE IN YOUR BAG!

ELLEN. They're around her wrist.

HOWARD. YOU DON'T NEED ANY KEYS —

ELLEN. *(Stepping up to her.)* Your keys are around your wrist. HERE. HERE. BUT YOU DON'T NEED THEM BECAUSE YOU'RE GOING TO STAY WITH US FROM NOW ON.

GLADYS. I don't want to go with you, I want to find my own apartment and I want to get a *job*!

ELLEN. WE CAN TALK ABOUT THAT LATER.

GLADYS. I don't understand where you're taking me!

HOWARD. You'll see where you are when you get there!

(HOWARD takes GLADYS out.)

GLADYS. *(Off.)* No! No! I don't want to go with you! I don't want to go!

(ELLEN shuts the door. Silence.)

ELLEN. Oy. All right. *(Pause.)* Do you have the lamp?

DANIEL. Yeah, you gave it to me this morning.

ELLEN. OK. And you don't want the … bureau, no, that's for Annie …

(Silence. ELLEN looks around the room.)

ELLEN. This place looks really dismal.

DANIEL. Are you gonna fix it up before you try to rent it? Or …

ELLEN. Oh yes, we have to, the whole ceiling looks like it's about to come down. *(Pause.)* I don't know. I feel so awful. I feel so dismal and hopeless. I don't know what's going to happen to her but I wish it would just happen. *(Pause.)* I know she always drove me crazy, but she was never a bad person. She was very loving. And she always wished me well.

DANIEL. I love you, Mom.

ELLEN. I love you too, sweetheart. *(She starts crying. They put their arms around each other.)* I came down here in the spring one time, and I caught up with her as she was on her way to the gallery ... and she was crawling along at a snail's pace, and her ankles looked so skinny, they were like *tooth*picks — and she just looked like this skinny old lady on the street, she looked as though a wind could blow her over.... She doesn't understand what's happening to her and neither do I.

DANIEL. Mom I love you so much I can't even tell you. I don't know what I'd do ...

(After a minute, she pulls away.)

ELLEN. All right. I don't want to leave poor Howard with her alone in the car.

DANIEL. All right, I'll see you for dinner tomorrow.

ELLEN. All right, sweetheart. Ay yai yai. Maybe we'll all survive. *(She kisses him. Pause.)* I think this really did me in. *(Pause.)* Let me know if you change your mind about the bureau.

DANIEL. OK, Mom, I'll see you tomorrow.

ELLEN. Good bye, sweetheart.

(She goes out. DANIEL comes forward.)

DANIEL. *(To the audience:)* Gladys moved in with Mom and Howard, where she just got worse and worse. For the last two months of her life all she did was moan, whether she was awake or asleep. A friend of mine said the whole thing was just unanswerable, and I guess it was. After she moved uptown I would see her when I went to visit, but I was out of it now.

My mother never got out. With the help of Howard, Florence and Marva she heroically stood by Gladys for the next two years. She took care of her and dressed her and cleaned her up and fed her and watched her fall apart, day in and day out with nothing to stop it and no relief in sight.

One night Mom called me up and told me she thought Gladys was dying. I rode my bike uptown and went into the back room where Gladys lived now. By that time she was just this tiny, eighty-seven year-old body, lying in the back of her daughter's apartment, hanging on with almost nothing, but struggling anyway for one more breath.

She finally died around two in the morning. And after that, it was a lot easier to remember what she was like before. But I never want to forget what happened to her. I want to remember every detail, because it really happened to her, and it seems like somebody should remember it.

It's not true that if you try hard enough you'll prevail in the end. Because so many people try so hard, and they don't prevail. But they keep trying. They keep struggling. And they love each other so much; it makes you think it must be worth a lot to be alive.

(He exits as the lights FADE OUT.)

THE END

A NOTE ABOUT SIMULTANEOUS DIALOGUE

For characters speaking to each other, dialogue laid out in side-by-side columns is meant to be spoken simultaneously. The actor saying the dialogue in the right column is not to wait for the actor saying the dialogue in the left column to finish, but to speak at the exact same time, taking his cue from the vertical placement of the text. For example:

CHARACTER A.	
What do you mean, speak at	
the same time? Didn't we —	CHARACTER B.
I am speaking at the same time …	He means speak simultaneously.
Well *you* didn't do it.	Don't wait for — That's not the
	point.

In the above, CHARACTER B says the word "He" at the same time that CHARACTER A says the word "I" and the word "Don't" at the exact same time CHARACTER A says the word "Well."

However, for double columns in which two sets of characters are having separate but simultaneous conversations, the speakers start at the same time, but continue along only in reference to their own column. For example:

CHARACTER A .	CHARACTER C.
I saw that movie yesterday.	What time does the bus get in?
CHARACTER B.	CHARACTER D.
Oh yeah? Was it good?	Five o'clock.
CHARACTER A.	CHARACTER C.
No, not especially.	The bus gets in at five o'clock?

In the above, CHARACTERS A and C start speaking at the same time, but then each column proceeds at its own pace, without reference to the other column.

While in come cases absolute precision is neither possible nor necessary, in general the more precisely the actors try to stick to these rules, the better the double dialogue will work.

COSTUME PLOT

ACT I	ACT II

GLADYS GREEN

Scenes 1, 2 & 3: Colorful blouse, dark pants, vest, tennis shoes, jewelry, glasses.

Scene 5: Polka dot blouse, dark pants, vest, tennis shoes.

Scene 1: Floral blouse, vest, light pants, tennis shoes.

Scene 2: Add hat.

Scene 3: Add purse.

Scene 4: Houserobe. Add hat, purse, dressy blouse, raincoat. Remove hat and raincoat.

Scene 5: Add coat.

ELLEN FINE

Scene 3: Dark sweater, light shell, dark pants, dark flats, jewelry.

Scene 4: Same pants and shoes with light cardigan set, purse, jewelry.

Scene 5: Change cardigan sweater for dark jacket. Change jewelry.

Scene 1: Light skirt, dark jacket, light shell, dark pumps, jewelry,

Scenes 2 & 3: Dark pants, dressy blouse, dark pumps, jewelry.

Scene 5: Light shell, light sweater, dark pants, black flats. Add jacket.

DANIEL REED

Scene 1: T-shirt, plaid button-down shirt, dark corduroy pants, glasses.

Scenes 3, 4 & 5: Dark jacket, dark T-shirt, dark corduroy pants.

Scenes 1, 2 & 3: Old jacket, black T-shirt, same pants.

Scene 4: Robe. Change to shorts. Change to tan cords and T-shirt.

Scene 5: Change to dark T-shirt.

ACT I	**ACT II**

HOWARD FINE

Scenes 3 & 4: Bright jacket, dark cardigan, bright pants, dark shoes.	*Scene 3:* Light shirt, bright pants, light pullover.
Scene 5: Oxford shirt, tie, dark pants, dark sport coat, dark shoes.	*Scene 5:* Dark flannel shirt, light pants, deck shoes.

DON BOWMAN

Scene 2: Dark jacket, T-shirt, dark pants, boots.	*Scene 2:* Dark blazer, light shirt, dark pants, Keds.
Scene 4: Dark sweater, jeans, paint rag.	*Scene 3:* T-shirt, jeans.
	Scene 4: Dark jacket, bright sweater, dark T-shirt, light pants, boots.

PROPERTIES:
TOP OF SHOW PRESET

ON STAGE

GALLERY
Table with assorted office supplies.
Armchair (R)
Chair (R)
Stool (L)
Chair (L)
Trash can
Easel
Ladder
Canvas

ELLEN'S DINING ROOM
4 chairs and table with place settings
Dresser
Wall sconce (plugged and straight)
Chair

ELLEN'S KITCHEN
Stool
Dog bowls
Cabinets with cookies, dishes, coffee, Chemex filters, coffee scoop
Counters w. Chemex coffee maker and assorted kitchen appliances
Refrigerator with ice cream in carton and 2 cans soda

STAGE RIGHT

Portfolio with paintings: wheelchair, wharf, mother, cardboard
Jar of hardware and brushes
Stack of boxes

STAGE LEFT

Armchair (Gladys)
Table
Lamp (plugged)
Large paper bag with coffee, tea, stirrers, etc.
2 sodas (1/3 full) with straw
Tray with 4 slices meatloaf and spatula
Divided bowl with mashed potatoes, vegetable and serving spoons
Salad bowl with lettuce and serving tongs
Bread basket with rolls
Plate with cheese, crackers, baby carrots and bowl of olives

PROPERTIES:
ACT II PRESET

ON STAGE

ELLEN'S LIVING ROOM
Sofa
Gladys' purse with lots of junk, in-
   cluding keys on wrist ban (2 hid-
   den)
End table
Chair
Chest
Standing lamp

(US) GLADYS' LIVING ROOM
(SR) Armchair
(SL) Chair
Triangular table with telephone
   (plugged), address book & pen
Magazine rack with dressing
Stack of stuff

GALLERY
Table with tablecloth, 4 cups,
   stack of cups, wine bottle with
   "wine," stack of napkins
Armchair
Gladys' hat
2 chairs
Stool
Easel
Ladder

STAGE RIGHT

Shopping bag
Ellen's purse with 2 sets of keys
Tray with saltines, cubed cheese
   and toothpicks

STAGE LEFT

Beer bottle (3/4 full)
Dresser
2 moving boxes
Folding chair
Key ring (Don)
Mugs with mint tea and decaf
Plate of cookies (repeat from
   Act I)

Set Plan/ACT I

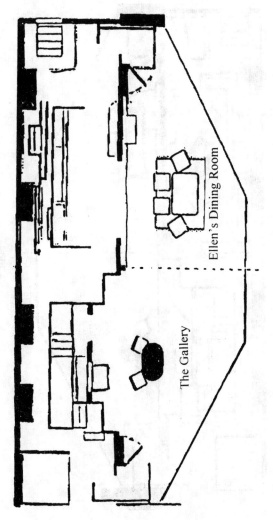

Ellen's Dining Room

The Gallery

Audience

Set Plan/ACT II

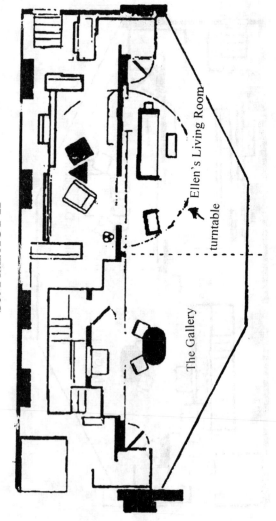

Ellen's Living Room

turntable

The Gallery

Audience

Set Plan/ACT II

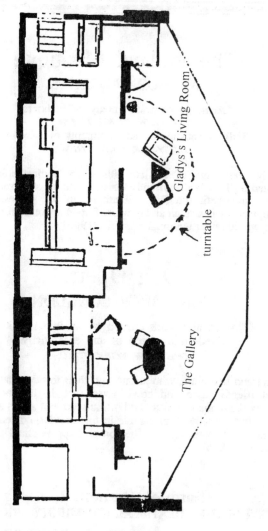

Gladys's Living Room

turntable

The Gallery

Audience

The Radical Mystique
ARTHUR LAURENTS

"Achingly earnest comedy of manners."
THE NEW YORK TIMES
"Full of caustic wit and moments of wisdom."
NEW YORK DAILY NEWS

In the New York of the late 60's when "radical chic" was coined by Tom Wolfe, friends Josie and Janice are arranging a party to benefit the Black Panthers. In the process, their complacency is shaken and they are forced to confront realities they would rather ignore. 3 m., 5 f. (#19961)

Dog Opera
CONSTANCE CONGDON

"A singular work created by an imagination
of redeeming freedom and eccentricity."
THE NEW YORK TIMES

Peter and Madeline, who are now in their thirities, have been best friends since childhood. Even though they are more loving than most couples and both in search of a partner, they are fundamentally incompatible in this moving contemporary comedy that premiered at The Joseph Papp Public Theatre. 5 m., 2 f. (#3866)

Samuel French, Inc.
SERVING THE THEATRICAL COMMUNITY SINCE 1830

DEATH DEFYING ACTS
David Mamet • Elaine May • Woody Allen

"An elegant diversion."
N.Y. TIMES
"A wealth of laughter."
N.Y. NEWSDAY

This Off-Broadway hit features comedies by three masters of the genre. David Mamet's brilliant twenty-minute play INTERVIEW is a mystifying interrogation of a sleazy lawyer. In HOTLINE, a wildly funny forty-minute piece by Elaine May, a woman caller on a suicide hotline overwhelms a novice counselor. A psychiatrist has discovered that her husband is unfaithful in Woody Allen's hilarious hour-long second act, CENTRAL PARK WEST. 2 m., 3 f. (#6201)

MOON OVER BUFFALO
Ken Ludwig

"Hilarious ... comic invention,
running gags [and] ... absurdity."
N.Y. POST

A theatre in Buffalo in 1953 is the setting for this hilarious backstage farce by the author of LEND ME A TENOR. Carol Burnett and Philip Bosco starred on Broadway as married thespians to whom fate gives one more shot at stardom during a madcap matinee performance of PRIVATE LIVES - or is it CYRANO DE BERGERAC? 4 m., 4 f. (#17)

Samuel French, Inc.
SERVING THE THEATRICAL COMMUNITY SINCE 1830